Mirror Lake

———❦———

GRACE COMSTOCK

Copyright © 2023 Grace Comstock.

All rights reserved. No part of this book may be reproduced, stored, or transmitted by any means—whether auditory, graphic, mechanical, or electronic—without written permission of both publisher and author, except in the case of brief excerpts used in critical articles and reviews. Unauthorized reproduction of any part of this work is illegal and is punishable by law.

ISBN: 979-8-89031-682-0 (sc)
ISBN: 979-8-89031-683-7 (hc)
ISBN: 979-8-89031-684-4 (e)

Because of the dynamic nature of the Internet, any web addresses or links contained in this book may have changed since publication and may no longer be valid. The views expressed in this work are solely those of the author and do not necessarily reflect the views of the publisher, and the publisher hereby disclaims any responsibility for them.

One Galleria Blvd., Suite 1900, Metairie, LA 70001
(504) 702-6708

In the Beginning...

Fred Wilder, his wife, Mabel, and their three boys, Fred Jr (17), William (15), and Jeffrey (13), bought 40 wooded acres on the outskirts of Mirror Lake, Montana on July 1, 1923. Everything they owned filled a horse-covered wagon. Over the next three days, more wagons arrived, rolling in one by one filled with women, children, livestock, and supplies. On the fourth day after the purchase, a set of three wagons arrived, one containing a dozen good strong men and the other two wagons carrying building materials for a house, barn, pavilion, and Church. Altogether, they numbered about 40 people: men, women and children. Fred referred to all of them on his property as "family". They kept to themselves, busily setting about building a homestead, chopping down and planking trees for the structures they wanted.

A huge plantation house quickly grew in a cleared area on the right side of the front four acres.

Painted dark green, the house had an enormous covered porch that wrapped around all sides of the house on both the first and second floor. A third story towered above the porch. Huge windows marked the rooms within on the first two floors. First floor had a huge kitchen, pantry, living room, dining room, gathering space, and several small servant's quarters along the back of the house. The second floor had 8 spacious bedrooms, and the third floor was an open spaced attic with a few storage rooms in two corners furthest from the stairs. A pretty little outhouse set off to the left side of the back door, and away from the house a little ways. Mabel painted it white and hung light green curtains in it.

The pavilion went up next a little ways from the house but not too far, essentially a cement floor furnished with picnic tables and a shingled roof suspended by poles in the center and the corners. Support poles were erected within the pavilion. The family gathered there for events. A regular barn was erected on the other side of the pavilion for the livestock.

About ten acres into the property, Fred and his fellow "family" members erected another building. Resembling a barn, it was twice the size with a peaked roof. They painted it bright red with bright white trim, and set an enormous white cross at the Apex of the gabled roof, above the double doors. The family only cleared some trees to erect the building and make a carriage road to it. The passage wound through the woods leisurely, a plain dirt road subject to the snowy winters and soggy springs of Montana. Automobiles were left at the house. Horse-drawn carriages were taken to the Church due to the road condition.

Quietly, Fred and his family made a living in the woods of Montana.

About 60 years ago

The old red barn sat quietly in the night on its ten acres. Not a cloud in the sky, the stars sparkled, and the bright moonlight from the full moon lit up the barn roof with a soft glow. The red paint was faded, a few of the boards were warped in spots, a state of being that Realtors called "weathered", yet it was a solid structure. The cross had been removed decades ago. A winding driveway swept gracefully through the property and ended at a paved parking lot to the left of the barn. A few cars dotted the space here and there. The inside was where it mattered.

Fred had been a farmer, but he was also the founder of the Ill Wind Coven. His barn was designed on the outside to look like ordinary barn, double doors in front, loft door on the second floor, but the inside was totally different. Members came and went through a smaller access door in the side of the barn.

The barn had two floors – the "dungeon" was smack in the middle of the first floor with a hallway surrounding it so that the Altar Room stood alone within the dungeon. The second "floor" had a half floor with a guard railing along it so nobody could walk off the edge. A railed stairway connected the two floors. No other rooms touched the Altar Room walls save for those small rooms that were inside the square space dedicated to the rituals and celebrations of the coven. Offices and workrooms were located under the second floor and had ceilings, the Alter Room did not. It was open to the roof of the barn, and was visible from all angles when looking down from the second floor. The alter room walls were painted matte black and absorbed light. Looking down on it, the openness didn't help.

An ominous space, the dungeon pulled light in and held it captive. Even looking at it from above, it was hard to make out anything moving within the space. Darkness lay over the room like a lid on a bowl. Straining your eyes, you might see silvery flecks moving within it like fish moving under the surface of a peaceful pool of water. Light directed into it from a flashlight didn't illuminate anything within the space, the beam of light just ended when it reached what would have been the ceiling of the room. No light reflected out of it either from the torches inside. It was as if the room was hiding its activities from the world. Members went in and back out hurriedly, as if they were wary of the space. Many of them mumbled to themselves about that room – as if evil emanated from it. Nobody lingered there unless they had too.

The Altar Room inside the "dungeon" was circular by design; 4 curving walls rose inside the square space, creating an inner circle where the coven participants gathered. The four curving walls opened once in each direction for an entrance/exit passageway. Each corner of the room between doorways sported leg chains and manacles used when torture was needed for a ritual. These hung from hooks set in the walls (six feet apart and a foot above the floor plus others placed in the walls well above 6 feet high) when not being used. Behind each set of chains was a door that swiveled open to reveal a small room. Two of these rooms were used for storage of coven regalia; the other two rooms were used for imprisoning ritual participants or punishing coven members for various infractions. There were no windows in these rooms, only a narrow opening along the top edge of the outer wall allowed air and slivers of light into the enclosed spaces so the captives were not in total darkness.

On the alter room floor, there was a circle painted in gold. Within the circle was a pentagram with symbols representing deities and rituals or festivals celebrated by the coven. Standing on the center of the pentagram was the alter. Made of marble, it had a solid base with a gold-filled pentagram etched in the surface. During the occasions of blood-letting, the grooves of the pentagram would collect the blood and channel it into containers for coven purposes.

Thankfully, those occasions were few and far between.

Halloween, 37 years ago – The Altar Room

Desmona whimpered as pain wracked her body. Her short blond hair clung to her scalp and her sweat-soaked skin glowed in the flickering torchlight. She wore only huge diaphanous scarfs in various pastel shades as a covering; the material draped over her gravid belly, spilling over the edges of the slab she lay on.

Desmona writhed on the altar, screaming as the pains increased, feet flat on the slab, hands spread open on either side of her belly and the child within, but the cold, black, gold-flecked marble had no give in it. Another pain peaked, and she screamed again. The scream echoed through the room, bouncing off the circular walls. The darkness closed in, intensifying the agony of the young woman.

Ethelinda raced to Desmona's side as another scream echoed off the circular walls of the altar room. A short, plump, matronly woman with short, dark-graying hair, she exuded an air of importance as she lay a hand softly on Desmona's forehead. Her light blue eyes shone with earnest as she said softly in a deep husky voice, "Hurry, child. The event must be done before this day ends." The kind hand lay on her forehead a moment, then was withdrawn. The soft torchlight was the only illumination in the room. One torch burned brightly in each corner of the alter room but only the alter was fully visible. The rest of the room was dark, the darkness contracting into the room as if waiting for the child to arrive.

Soft rustlings in the room bespoke of other members present even though Desmona could not see them. Wearily, she raised her head, straining to see anyone in the darkness beyond the torchlight. Vague shapes swam just beyond her vision, the torchlight making them seem like ghosts. A low-muted chant began.

In that darkest hour, when the wind howls
the wolves speak, the language of men garbles
He will walk among us

In appearance everyone, in actual fact no one
unborn by woman, unfathered by man
He that walks among us

The faithful rewarded, the treacherous shall die
a virgin he'll plunder in that darkest hour
when He walks among us

She dropped her head back on the altar, exhausted. Her muscles cramped, and she shrieked, her body pulling in on itself as if suctioned in, her hands digging vainly at the gold pentagram etched in the marble. The pressure broke, and she screamed again, her hands gripping the edges of the slab she was on so tight her knuckles turned white. A monster cramp tore at her, her pelvic bones spread, her legs locked in the birthing position and amidst a huge gush of blood, a baby emerged. Desmona slumped into a heap as a wail rent the air from the new life.

Ethelinda caught the child and wrapped it in a soft pastel pink blanket. Carrying the bundle carefully, she approached the head of the alter, crooning softly to the child to soothe it. A big man emerged from the shadows between two of the torches and stood at the head of the alter, meeting Ethelinda.

A hooded black robe covered him head to foot, the oversized hood, flipped up, covered his head and his face. He held a decorated oak staff in his right hand that towered two feet above his height. Various medals, mandalas and pendants were wrapped around the staff under the head and hung down the shaft on chains or cords, but none of them reached his hand. His fingernails were filed to a point like talons and painted black. He was well over 6 feet tall and broad shouldered. His thick fingers gripped the staff tighter as the midwife drew closer.

"My Lord Lachlan," Ethelinda said softly, her head bowed, "the child is a girl." She held the child up so he could see her. The baby kicked and waved her arms. The blanket fell away, exposing the naked child to the night air. She shivered and mewled in the sudden coolness but did not cry. She lay quietly in the midwife's hands, staring into the black eyes of the High Priest with her own startling blue eyes, blond hair sticking out every which way from her birth, her arms and legs still.

"Human?" Lachlan asked, his baritone voice quiet and commanding. He moved the hood back so he could examine the child before him. His black eyes sparkled in the torchlight, the flickers from the torches shimmered in his coal black hair, so black it showed blue in torchlight. His eyes traveled the child's body from top to bottom as if looking for faults.

"It appears so, my lord," Ethelinda said, softly. She withdrew the child from his scrutiny, wrapping her in the blanket again. She waited, as if for orders, standing before the High Priest with the child in her arms. She bounced the child a little to keep her quiet while she waited.

Lachlan's attention was drawn to the altar as Desmona screamed again. Ethelinda scurried back to altar and lay the child next to her mother. The child wailed loudly, one hand breaking free from the blanket and waving in the air. Desmona whimpered.

"Another child comes, my lord," Ethelinda said, her voice soft but strong. She had hurriedly moved to the foot of the altar and gripped Desmona's ankle. "Push, child! Push!" The young mother screamed in agony, her body arching off the altar. Holding this position for a few seconds, she slumped back onto the unforgiving stone, breathing heavily and whimpering. A single pastel blue scarf slipped off her middle and drifted to the floor. The chanting grew a little louder in volume, and the child on the altar fell quiet.

Ethelinda grabbed another soft blanket, this one pastel lavender, and wrapped the new child in it. Thumping the feet, she smiled slightly as the child wailed lustily. Picking it up, she brought the baby to Lachlan.

Kneeling, she opened the blanket, exposing the child and held her up a bit so the priest could see her. Startling blue eyes met black ones. The child flinched and screamed, arms and legs waving as if fighting off an attacker.

"Another girl, my lord," Ethelinda said, her head bowed, and murmured, "identical twin girls." Defensively, she brought the screaming child back down, wrapping the blanket around her, and hunched over her. Desmona groaned on the altar, the sister lay quietly as if listening. Another scarf, this one pastel green, slipped off the mother and floated lazily to the floor.

"Human?" Lachlan asked again, his voice louder and clear. His eyes sought confirmation, but Ethelinda's body shielded the second child from his sight. He knocked the staff on the floor in irritation, the feathers at the top jolting as the staff hit the floor. *One, two, three.*

"Yes, my Lord." Ethelinda turned away, placing the baby in a bassinet off in the gloom away from the altar. She returned almost immediately and picked up the first-born, carrying her off in the same direction. She clucked to the children, her soft ticking sounding disembodied in the gloom, then returned to the mother's side. The babies lay next to each other, face to face for a few minutes, then the pink one shoved the lavender one away and both cried for a minute, then fell quiet.

"Please," Desmona whispered. She still lay prone on the alter. Her hands fluttered weakly in the torchlight. They fell back gracefully unto the alter as Ethelinda crooned to her.

"Shh. Be quiet now. They sleep." Ethelinda covered the young woman with the scarfs and helped her move into a more comfortable position. Wringing out a soft lilac and chamomile scented cloth taken from a shallow bowl, Ethelinda began wiping down Desmona's skin. The coolness felt wonderful to the young woman, who inhaled, letting the scent relax her, and closed her eyes.

"Cease." Lachlan stepped into the light and flipped his hood down again. He moved to the side of the Altar, gesturing Ethelinda back. She bowed her head, dropped the cloth back into the bowl, and stepped back into the circle surrounding the altar. She heard the children fuss but they remained quiet.

Lachlan stared down into Desmona's eyes, his own face unreadable. She trembled and hugged herself. Lachlan gestured to the shadows, and turned towards the figure who approached.

A small woman came and stood before him, everything but her hands hidden by a black robe. She was about 5 feet tall. The hood wrapped around her head, the opening shrouding her face in darkness. Long-boned fingers with short manicured fingernails painted black gracefully folded together and disappeared inside the sleeves of the robe, so all that was standing in front of him was a very small figure robed in black, completely hidden from him.

"Metis," Lachlan said, his tone commanding, "Check the children and use your discernment. You must determine if the ritual was successful." His eyes bored into Desmona's face. She paled when he mentioned the children, and her trembling became more visible.

"Yes, my lord." Metis' voice was low pitched, and scratchy, as if she didn't use it much. She took one step toward the bassinet, then stopped and turned back. "You will hold me blameless regardless of the findings?"

"If you say true, no blame shall be yours." Lachlan said, waving his hand dismissively. His eyes stayed on Desmona. She nervously began to fidget.

"Thank you, lord." Metis bowed and left the light. She glided over the rough surface of the stone floor until she was hanging over the bassinet. She stretched out a hand over the first-born girl, and closed her eyes. She waved her fingers slightly over the child. The coven fell silent, the atmosphere disturbed only by Desmona's whimpers of pain from the altar. Metis opened her eyes. "Human," she said, her voice cracking. Clearing her throat she said, louder, "Strictly human. Even the blood coursing through the veins is mostly human. This child is of little use to us."

The coven murmured, a flurry of many voices spoke as one, then quieted again. Desmona moaned in the sudden silence. One of the torches flared and died, plunging the dungeon further into gloom. Someone gasped, and was quickly silenced. A 'click' relit the torch. Once it flickered brightly along with the rest, Metis stretched her hand out over the second child, pulling it back almost immediately with a startled yip. Holding it up, she inspected it in the gloom. Rubbing it with her other hand, she shook it then wiped it on her robe.

"This child is human, too, my lord, but her blood burns with the demon's touch. She is pure enough to be useful to us." Metis said. Her soft scratchy voice bounced off the walls. She rubbed her hand on her robe as if to rub out the itch from the demonic blood of the child.

Desmona began to scream. "No!" She struggled to get off the altar, throwing off the scarves encasing her and trying to swing her legs off the edge and sit up. "Leave my daughters alone!"

Lachlan swooped Desmona's body with an outstretched hand. She tensed and fell back onto the alter with a *thump*, stiffening as orange light glowed over her body, jerking violently then quieting as it sunk in, paralyzing her. She lay sprawled on the altar, one leg slung off the edge already while the other poised, cocked as if ready to swing off the edge so she could stand, her eyes pleaded with him. She tried vainly to move and not a part of her budged. He turned away from Desmona, gripping his staff so hard his knuckles turned white, leaving her in that position. "What tainted the ceremony, Metis?"

Metis closed her eyes and raised her arms to the ceiling, palms up and open. She swayed in the dim light as she concentrated, then her body went rigid and her eyes flew open. "Hakon says the vessel was not pure. This impurity destroyed the covenant."

Lachlan jerked slightly, face pale. His eyes flashed in the darkness. He closed his fist over Desmona, and her body bucked wildly, banging her head violently against the altar. With a final sigh, she was dead. Lachlan swooped his hand again she settled back onto the altar, arms at her sides and legs straight. A sheet materialized over her, dropping gently down and settling over the body.

"What does our Lord wish we do with the children?" Lachlan asked, turning back to Metis.

A filmy ribbon of energy swirled up from the floor like a sparkly water from a fountain and twirled around Metis until she was completely surrounded by it. The ectoplasm drew in closer to Metis, pulsing and rippling like a garment settling itself on her. She gasped, hands flying to her throat, garbled sounds escaping her lips. She crumpled to the ground as the blue mist sunk in. The coven murmured.

"Silence!" Lachlan thundered. "Move now and die." He dropped to one knee and bowed his head, right hand on the staff. His staff stood erect and towered over him. He pulled it closer and leaned against it while he crouched on the cement floor.

Metis came into the light, but she was no longer totally human. Her skin was tinged blue. The robes didn't quite fit her anymore; they strained at the seams, and instead of dainty little feet large cloven hooves peeked out and clacked on the floor with each step. *Clock, clock, clock.* Pointy ram's horns grew from her head, up and flaring out, and her eyes were yellow with vertical black irises. Her fingers were longer than normal and ended in sharp yellow talons. Her nose widened and flattened, yet poked out more, sharp teeth protruded from the makeshift snout. Cro-magnum eyebrows completed the alteration. Remnants of her Asian features were apparent in the face that swept the coven, and each pair of eyes dropped before the figure could settle on one. "Who chose the vessel?" a deep voice boomed from the slight figure.

Lachlan trembled and said, low, "I did, my lord." His head dropped further, and his grip tightened on the staff. He closed the hand not gripping the staff into a fist, driving the sharpened nails into his palm. He winced.

Hakon/Metis let out a primal scream toward the ceiling, a deep-throated bellow, cords in his neck standing out like ropes, hands open and down, fingers spread and curved up as if he were holding something heavy. He stomped the ground with his right hoof and blue flames shot from his hands in streams, wafting up to the top of the room and swirling in a circle just under the lid of darkness hovering over the Altar Room. The fire gathered into a ball and streamed down, diving for Lachlan and engulfed him completely, contracting around him and releasing as if breathing. The more intense the color of the flame, the more intense the agony. Lachlan writhed on the floor, fighting to voice no sound. His staff trembled, feathers shivering from the vibrations of his grip but didn't drop as he endured the displeasure of his deity. The coven watched, silent but wide-eyed, as their leader groveled.

Hakon withdrew the flame to swirl around the ceiling again, and Lachlan slumped to the floor, breathing heavily. His staff clattered on the ground next to him. Lachlan sobbed. "I'm sorry, my lord," he stammered, beginning to move slightly. Lachlan licked his lips. They were dry. He tested parts of his body to make sure they still worked. The fire had been so intense he was afraid he'd lost parts of himself to it. Thankfully everything seemed like it was still there and functional. Lachlan drew a sigh of relief.

Hakon chuckled. "I love a good fire, don't you?" The blue-tinged figure walked to the altar, his hooves clacking on the marble floor. He examined the lifeless body on it, then turned around and leaned against the tabletop, his back to the remains of the young woman, facing the coven leader. He cocked his head to the side, crossed his feet at the ankles, and crossed his arms over his chest.

"So, Lachlan, what do we do with your bungled offerings?" He clicked a talon against his teeth. "I had such plans for this day. Finally, a son to call my own. I had his education all planned out, his coming of age ceremony planned, and even was picking out upholstery for his throne. I make all this effort," he swept an arm in front of him in a semi-circle, palm up, "and what do I find? A GIRL - and not one but TWO!" Hakon bounced a blue fireball off Lachlan's chest, and laughed as the blue orb came back to him. As if by agreement, one baby whimpered while the other cooed as the demon's laughter echoed off the walls.

Lachlan was knocked over backwards from the force of the orb, and just lay there, panting. "Please, lord..." he said, his voice breaking. He rolled over to his side, trying to pull himself back on his feet. He reached out and felt around for his staff.

"Still, I suppose it wasn't your fault, now was it?" Hakon drawled, stomping a hoof impatiently. "Mortal man can't exactly choose the sex of children conceived, now can he? Of course, I can. I'll have to think about this." He continued, stomping the hoof on the floor in an uneven beat while he thought. "Well, truthfully, a pure vessel would have birthed sons. Chips off the ol' horn, so to speak."

Lachlan felt his head pound each time the hoof hit the floor. He could barely see his staff, but somehow managed to reach out and grasp it. Using its length, he pulled himself up from the floor until he was standing more or less upright. Small hot flashes radiated out from his chest, and suddenly he didn't feel so well.

"We will do as you command, lord." Lachlan gasped. He struggled to remain upright. He broke out in a cold sweat.

"All in due time, Lachlan. All in due time." Hakon said, calmly, holding up a hand so the palm faced Lachlan. The demon was staring at the sheet-covered body on the altar, and his eyes narrowed.

Lachlan stood silent, leaning on the staff. The hot flashes seemed to be easing some, thankfully. He pulled a hand across his forehead and stood staring at it. It was so wet a drop of condensation fell from his palm and splashed on the floor, blossoming out like a flower opening. *How beautiful*, he thought as he dried his hands on his robe. His master's voice drew his attention back to the altar.

Hakon stared at him a moment, then stopped stomping his foot and turned to the altar. Laying a hand on the forehead of Desmona's body, he crooned, "Yes, daughter, it wasn't your fault, either, was it? Death seems like such a strange reward for your services."

He knew, Lachlan thought. His knees began to knock, so swiftly did the trembling start.

Immediately his body flushed and he broke out again in a cold sweat. His palm was so damp his hand slipped down the staff despite his grip tightening.

Hakon swept back the sheet, and held a hand over Desmona's heart. "Rise, my child, and bear witness to me." A small blue orb shot from his palm and settled over the young woman's chest. It swirled for a moment, then sank in.

Desmona's body began to tremble, then shake. She jerked about, then she moved, obviously trying to sit up. Hakon reached out and helped her, swinging her legs over the edge of the altar and assisting her to a sitting position. She opened her eyes and stared at Hakon for a second, wavering slightly, then Lachlan. Her eyes glowed with blue fire; her hair stuck up every which way. She was unnaturally still, and there was no breath.

"Speak, child. Tell them what went wrong with the ritual." Hakon commanded, waving a hand toward Lachlan. Lachlan felt his heart lurch in his chest, and gripped his staff closer.

"He came," Desmona said, her voice toneless. "He visited me in the night." Her blue eyes slowly moved back to Hakon's face and remained there. Slight sparks showed blue fire. It was the only sign of life in her. One of the babies mewled. Desmona remained staring at Hakon, ignoring her child.

"Who did?" Hakon asked. He drummed his fingers against his thigh while he listened to the reanimated woman in front of him.

Lachlan's legs almost gave out, and if it weren't for the grip he had on his staff, he would have fallen. *She was going to tell.* He had a wild urge to run and his body tensed as if it were going to do just that.

"Lachlan." Desmona said, her voice expressionless. "He came to me before the ritual." Her head swiveled haphazardly towards Lachlan and she stared at him for a second or two, then her gaze moved back to Hakon. She moved unnaturally, in little jerky movements. In order to move her head to the side, she had to tip it that way and move the rest of her under it to look straight at something.

"Did he say what his purpose was?" Hakon asked, nailing Lachlan with a glance. His hands tightened into fists at his side. He visibly relaxed, then flexed his hands, opening and closing his fists while staring at Lachlan. Lachlan paled but stood strong, lifting his head defiantly.

"To prepare me, he said. He promised wonderful things would happen if you were pleased." Her eyes closed and Desmona wilted, collapsing in a heap on top of the altar. Hakon tenderly placed her back in a resting position and covered her with the sheet again, then turned his back on her, leaning on the altar facing Lachlan. He crossed his arms over his chest.

"So," he said. Hakon glanced at the sheet-covered body. "I suppose you killed her to save your own miserable life, Lachlan. You knew the rules." He sighed mightily.

Lachlan gripped his staff tighter. "I was attempting to make the ritual a success, master." The crystal ball on the end of his staff began to glow as he summoned his power. He stood straighter in defense, as if straightening his spine would stop the trembling. He felt an acute sense of doom. *This must be what it means to 'fall into despair',* he thought.

"Yes. That's what we both wanted, wasn't it?" Hakon waved his hand at the staff, and the light went out. The demon grinned at him, sharp pointy fangs glowing pure white in the blue tinged skin. "I don't suppose you remembered that she had to be a virgin to ensure success? And even though both children are mine, their mother not being a virgin tainted them. Neither is pure."

Lachlan found himself speechless, staring at those fangs in fascination. Of course he knew that. He was the one who found the ritual in an ancient book, and the one who had enacted it again after 300 years. But she had been so enticing… abruptly, he brought his attention back to his master. He knew them teeth were important - he just couldn't figure out why…

"Which leaves us with two children who are effectively useless to our purpose." Hakon snapped his fingers, interrupting Lachlan's thoughts. Hakon thrust his right palm towards Lachlan and orange flame shot out, engulfing Lachlan and incinerating him in an instant. With one agonized shriek, Lachlan was gone. His staff clattered to the floor. Hakon threw his head back and laughed mightily, holding his stomach and chuckling in glee. The coven members witnessing the attack whimpered but dared not move lest they draw attention to themselves. They stood silent during Hakon's laughter.

Abruptly he stopped and cocked his head. Listening for a second, he said, "Now comes the time for me to leave." He began to turn to blue smoke, and as he disappeared, he said, "Bury the mother. Send the first born to an orphanage, and nurture the second born. When she comes of age, show her the ritual. I will contact her then with further instructions. And remember, my children, I am always watching." A burst of flame, and he was gone.

Metis' body thumped to the floor, lifeless, making a total of two bodies for cleanup. Lachlan's staff lay on the floor, lost without its owner. A black spot on the floor was the only thing left of Lachlan. From that day forward, no matter how hard someone scrubbed at it, the mark never faded nor went away.

The coven stood still for a while, as if waiting for a sign. Nobody cried for the dead; it was as if they were afraid to draw attention to themselves even by mourning fallen members. It wasn't until the voice of their new leader cried from her bassinet that the people began to move.

Four male members carried the bodies of the young mother and Metis to the cemetery on the grounds. There would not be funerals for them, neither died in good graces. A female picked the staff up and carried it to the High Priest's office. Leaning it against the wall inside the room, she left hurriedly, pulling the door shut behind her.

When they got a new High Priest, he would know what to do with it.

The first-born daughter was taken to the next state and left on the steps of a hospital. A woman named Harriet Knightshade, a temporary employee from a local employment agency, worked there in the billing office. Arriving early, Harriet picked up the blond, blue eyed little girl and carried her into the hospital, intending to give the child to the maternity ward until her parentage could be discovered and she could be reunited with her parents.

When Harriet entered the hospital carrying the baby, everyone she met cooed over the baby and told her what a lucky mom she was to have such a beautiful child. One patient, a little old lady with dementia, swept up to Harriet and clasping both her hands, told her that God gave Harriet that beautiful child and she should take the greatest care of her because the child would save the world someday. Harriet thanked her, and the woman smiled softly, went back into her room, lay on the bed, and immediately died.

After the death, Harriet went back to her office, taking the child with her. Bundling her coat up, she stuffed it in a bottom drawer and lay the child in it, keeping an eye on her during the morning hours. The baby cooed and played with her fingers while Harriet worked away. She borrowed a few diapers and a bottle and formula from the maternity ward until she could get supplies. It was a pleasant morning.

From that moment on, Harriet Knightshade was a mother. She prayed and thanked God for the child, for Harriet was truly unique.

She was 37, a virgin, and had no interest at all in men or sex. She knew that if she had a child, it would be because God gave her one.

And he did.

A week later, the local news station reported that a local woman was struck and killed by a runaway bus while on her way to work. Upon investigation of the woman's apartment, police found evidence of a child, but not the child itself. Routinely, they knocked on the doors of her neighbors, both giving them the news that Harriet had met her demise and to see if they could dig up anything about the child.

The investigating officers found the child holed up with an elderly neighbor, who didn't know anything about the child other than Harriet telling her the little girl belonged to a dead cousin. No, she didn't hear Harriet talk about anyone else regarding the child. Upon further investigation, the officers discovered there literally WAS nobody who could or would take the child in. Harriet had nobody on the face of the planet, literally no family to speak of at all, and that left the child in a precarious position.

Social services took over the case, trying their best to find a home for such a pretty baby. Until such a paradise could be found, the little girl waited at the local orphanage. In vain.

CHAPTER ONE

Topics for the New Millennium was one of the few talk shows hosted out of a local TV station in Bozeman, MT. Tucked behind the City Hall building, The TV station used a small, on-premises recording studio to reach its audience. The broadcast covered the surrounding area, including the community of Mirror Lake itself.

Inside the studio, along the back wall, pleated midnight blue curtains hung from ceiling to floor. A white-framed, midnight blue cloud-shaped sign hung in the middle of the curtain with "Topics for the New Millennium" in white scripted across it. Eggshell blue plush carpeting lay on the floor. The interview area in front of the curtain sported light blue, comfortable, overstuffed chairs surrounding a polished wooden-framed coffee table. An elegant, dainty, Chinese tea service on a silver serving tray set on the jade green top. A teapot steamed invitingly.

Just behind the host's chair stood a staff. The staff was about 6 feet tall, with esoteric symbols carved into the shaft. A Wizard's face was carved into the top of the staff. The expression on the carved face was that of a stern taskmaster, giving the staff an air of all business. Jason connected with this staff on a personal level, and never did a broadcast without it. Most of the time it just stood there in mute testimony, presiding over the room as if keeping watch.

Very little was in the room other than the furniture and stage fixtures seen on camera. Thick wires flowed from the cameras and lined the floor everywhere you looked, duck taped down to avoid accidents until the floor looked like a road map to nowhere. The soundproof control booth was off in the corner. People moved around inside it, silent to all watching. Cameramen stayed silent and almost motionless, moving only to adjust their cameras during the broadcast.

The director gave the countdown to start and pointed at the host.

"Welcome to 'Topics for the New Millennium.' I'm your host, Jason Dooley." A short, stocky, darkly-tanned, dark-haired man addressed the studio camera. His startling blue eyes bored into the lens. "Today's guest is Lillian Wassanbloom, known in the psychic circuit as Madame Selena. Welcome, Lillian."

Jason Dooley stood five feet eight inches in his stocking feet. He worked out three times a week at a gym in Virginia City. As a result, he positively bulged into his frame. There was no fat on him anywhere. Today he wore dark slacks, dark deck shoes, and a lavender-hued silk shirt open at the neck and rolled up his arms. His nails were buffed and manicured. His short black hair was spiked with gold powder on the tips, creating a soft golden aura that surrounded his head in the pastel glow from the ceiling spot lights. Blue, pink, yellow, and white overhead spotlights combined to create a goldenish glow in the camera room, and the gold tips really stood out on the camera. He cradled a clipboard on his lap, holding it steady on his knees with his left hand.

"Thanks, Jason. I'm happy to be here." Lilly said, crossing her legs and clasping her hands loosely together in her lap. She smiled at him. "You can call me Lilly." She wore an electric blue pheasant blouse, scoop necked and elasticized at the wrists with a short, ruffled edge to the sleeve, and belted at the waist. The belt she wore was rainbow hued, and clasped at the front with a rainbow shaped buckle. She had pushed her sleeves up to her elbows. She wore a loose-fitting floor-length skirt, earthy brown in color, with dark blue ankle boots. Ankle socks hidden in the boots allowed her bare legs to peak out from under the skirt. She wore a large crystal pendent and a single small, silver angel-wing earring in her left ear. She had an ear wrap on the right side that wrapped around her ear and drooped a few small colored stones on the right side in front of her ear and another silver angel-wing behind on the back side of the wrap. For all that she looked the part, she felt like a fake sitting there, and glanced off to the side of the host to the man in the audience for reassurance.

Randy James sat off to the side, smiling at her every time she looked his way. She was glad. He was such a godsend! She'd met him about a year ago. He'd come into her insurance agency, looking for full coverage on his truck. She'd guided him to a policy that wouldn't soak him an arm and a leg for liability, since he hauled work materials in his truck. He built houses, "Just like Jesus," he'd said, and laughed. She'd laughed too.

He'd called her the next day and invited her to lunch. He was tall, wiry but solid, and a total doll in her opinion. He looked just like that irritable doctor character from the TV right down to the hair and eye color. Thank God that's where the resemblance ended. His charm and grace touched her and they'd spent the afternoon in her bed. The charisma that rolled off him attracted her like a moth to a flame; she lusted after him all the time. She smiled a little. Maggie would say he knocked her socks off. Her smile faltered a tiny bit. Actually, her daughter wouldn't say anything of the kind. Maggie was a Gothic kinda gal.

Lilly wrenched her mind back to the business at hand. She shifted her position a little, settling into the deep cushion of the chair. A crystal ball on a dragon stand sat on a small round display table to her right, a magician statue she'd gotten from a catalog posed next to it. She had brought them because they insisted on coming with her. *Always listen to your tools*, her teacher had once said long ago. *You never know when you're going to need them, but they do.* She listened.

Jason smiled at her and lay the clipboard on the coffee table. He picked up the teapot. Tipping it towards her, her "asked" if she would like some. She nodded yes. "Thanks, Lilly. Today's topic is witchcraft. Some people would say that's what you practice. Would you agree with them?" He poured two cups of tea from the pot and set one in front of her on a saucer.

"Not at all, Jason." Lilly met his eyes with her own blue ones, and leaned forward, picking up the cup and leaving the saucer on the table. Sitting back, she cuddled the cup in her hands, shifting her grip a little while waiting for the cup to cool off. Steam rose from the cup, and her mouth watered. She swallowed. "I am not a witch in the historical sense of the word. I am a psychic." She tossed her long blond hair out of her face and sipped her tea.

"Some people see no difference," Jason commented, smiling at the camera. He crossed his ankles and picked up his own cup, sipped it and set it back down on the saucer. He had warned her earlier while they were going over the content of the show that sometimes his guests got uncomfortable with the directness of his "assaults," as he called them. She distinctly got the feeling he saw himself as an investigative reporter searching for the truth, uncovering it like rolling boulders out of the way to find it, sometimes amidst the "webs of deceit" people weave around themselves.

"True enough." Lilly agreed. She grinned at him as if daring him to start something. A sense of feeling trapped ticked at her mind. She ignored it.

"So, what would you say is the difference?" Jason asked. He reached behind his chair and pulled his staff closer, as if it had ears and could follow the conversation. Poising the face so that it looked at her, he sat back in the chair and grinned at her expectantly.

Lilly looked away from the staff towards the faces of the crew and saw genuine interest. She placed her teacup back on the saucer in front of her and laced her hands together in her lap. "Well, I guess you could say the basic difference between a witch and a psychic is the intent behind the motive. A witch does not have to be a psychic to practice the craft, although she or he could become one. Many of them work on developing their "powers" to boost their results when spellcasting, potion making, or mediating." Lilly shrugged a little, indicating to each their own. "I daresay their job would be easier if they were, but it is not necessary. A psychic is either born with his or her doors wide open, so to speak, or spends time developing those abilities. However, no matter how the abilities are developed, or even if they are there or not makes no difference. Intent and purpose is everything in this line of work." She fussed with hem of her blouse, smoothing it with her hands, then forced herself to stop lest it show her nervousness.

"What would the intent be for each?" Jason said, pouring them each more tea.

"For the purpose of our discussion, we will assume that all physics have innate, or inborn, abilities. These psychics embrace their abilities with the intent of helping mankind, whether they know it or not. Practice makes perfect with psychics, and the more they use their abilities they better they become. However, most can't use their abilities for their own personal gain. There are many different ways a psychic can use to communicate with the other side," Lilly said. "The concept is really confusing with a lot of different paths one can travel, but no matter what path you walk most people need to practice to perfect it. There are too many levels within the subject to explain it more adequately in the time slot we have. I could talk for the entire show about psychic abilities and how to develop them."

"I understand. What about witchcraft?" Jason picked up a tarot deck from the floor and opened it, pulling the cards out of the box and placing the deck face down on the coffee table. Lily glanced at it, then looked back at Jason.

"Witchcraft has several aspects, too. Most witches exist within a coven, which gives them the benefit of practicing their craft with like-minded people. Some believe this gives more power to spells and rituals due to more minds focused on the same task, and some use the experience to learn how to properly cast spells. Spells and rituals never happen without a pattern, and most of them have specific operating instructions. Fledgling witches, known as "novices," require instructions. I'm not saying that all witches belong to a coven, because they don't. Solitary practitioners are becoming more and more popular everyday. There are benefits to each kind of practice, but a group of like minds can usually affect change on a larger scale or within a quicker time frame. A witch with some psychic ability is a bigger asset to her craft, whether in a coven or no. That's why most witches try to develop their abilities." Lily glanced up at the staff, then fixed her gaze back on Jason. The face on it made her nervous, like the silly thing was staring at her.

"What about the concept of good and evil?" Jason asked, his eyes flashing. He picked up his clipboard again and lay it face up on his lap.

"There is no such distinction in the spirit world, Jason. Events are not good or evil. Only what people do with them makes them one or the other. I'd love to tell you about good and bad covens, etc, but they just don't exist." Lilly said sadly. "That's probably not what you and your audience wants to hear, but it's essentially true. A coven doesn't start out as good or evil, it becomes one or the other by the actions of it's members."

"What about those movies that show evil covens trying to raise demons? Hollywood had to get those ideas from somewhere. Are you saying that's just propaganda invented to sell movie tickets?" Jason asked. He slapped the clipboard with an open palm and steadied it as it rocked. "What kind of things can a coven do anyway? Can they hex people? I can't even begin to tell you how many phone messages and emails I get from people that think they are cursed."

"A lot of questions, Jason. Regarding Hollywood and their take on raising up demons by witchcraft, that surely is propaganda. There's lots of interesting ideas in that town, but what comes out in movies is designed to make money not spread the truth, or even tell the truth about most things. If you looked at those plans to raise the devil in reality they would never work out. They never do in the movies, and they wouldn't in real life. Precision is the key to most rituals - if everything is not "perfect" it doesn't work right. Simple as that. Usually it goes badly for whomever tries it." Lilly laughed, but not unkindly. "Regarding the curses, and the people thinking that they are cursed, well, they are in a sense. Their thoughts create the curse for them."

"Are you saying that everyone out there," Jason gestured towards the camera lens and the people beyond, "listening to us who thinks they are suffering a "curse" is psychologically disturbed?"

"Not at all. I'm saying that the human mind can produce any phenomena you suggest to it. The human mind is like a computer." Lillian leaned on her knees with her elbows, lacing her fingers together in front of her as if praying, then picked up her cup and sat back in the chair again. "It is literal. If you can convince it of something, that something comes to be, no matter what it is. Thoughts are things."

"I don't get it." Jason stated. His entire manner fairly screamed it at her. The cameraman pointed at the clock. Jason glanced at it, then back to her, obviously expecting her to explain herself. "I am sure I am not the only one struggling with this. Can you give us an example please?" The cameraman raised his hands up and dropped them back to his sides as if to say *I tried to go to a commercial.* Jason ignored him.

Lilly stared at Jason for a second, then said, "Let's use the curse you've mentioned as an example in the following story: Once upon a time, a young woman named Susan lived in a small rural village next to a wooded area. An evil witch supposedly lived in the woods, and rumor had it she religiously cursed trespassers with various afflictions. Boils, rashes, seizures, fits, sudden unexplained illnesses, the list was endless. Residents left the woods be lest they incur the wrath of the witch. While walking one day, Susan was lost in thought and accidentally entered the trailing edge of those woods. She didn't notice where she was for a short while, but when she did she hastily vacated the woods and went straight home. She not seen a soul on her walk.

The next day, in the town square, people talked. Word was the witch was seen the night before and the villagers were scared. They all wondered who the witch was coming after. Susan was just as scared. What if there really was a witch, and the witch saw her while she was in the woods? Susan cringed in her house all that night, hoping the witch didn't see her. She finally fell asleep, but did not rest well. Her "guilt" was already weighing on her mind.

The next morning, a symbol normally associated with the witch had been etched into Susan's front door. She collapsed upon seeing it and had to be sedated. She spent the next few days petrified and in hysterics, terrified the witch would come and get her, until she finally stiffened into a seizure and died. What would you say was the underlying cause of death?" Lily asked Jason.

"Obviously self-inflicted. End of story." Jason said, smugly.

"From the doctor's standpoint, you'd be correct. Official cause of death would be heart failure. However, let's look back at that community, and review the "curse" angle," Lily said. "First, look at the "facts" if you will. We have a superstitious community with a consequential legend in place. That kind of legend is one that inflicts terrible things on those people who tempt it. This one is about an evil witch that curses trespassers if you enter her territory, and we have someone who did just that." Lily leaned forward a little with the intensity of her thoughts, and her desire to express herself.

"Now, the community believes in the curse, and so does Susan. The belief is there, all someone needs to do is kickstart it. The scene at the public square firmly sets the seed in Susan's mind that YES - 1) the witch is abroad 2) Someone was out there and 3) someone is going to get it. The next day, when the symbol shows on her door, it is "proof" the witch saw her, and Susan begins to "feel" the curse working in her. All that is required on her behalf is belief." Lilly noted his look of fear with satisfaction and continued.

"Ok, now, once convinced, the job is done. We don't need to do a single thing more. Her guilty conscience does the rest. In Susan's case, her mind carried out it's directive, she believed she was cursed, so therefore everything she did turned out badly. Even if she poopooed the idea in the first place," Lily waved her hand dismissively as if to say, 'go on', "the seed was planted and her mind did the rest. Her mind enacted the curse without any further input from anyone. She was convinced that someone had taken control of her life, and lo and behold! It happened." Lily set her cup back on the saucer and continued, "For some people, this is enough to convince themselves of bad luck, and someone else causing it through a curse or a hex. People will spend thousands of dollars on charlatans to remove the curse they think they have - and all along it was their own mind sabotaging them." Lilly sat back in her chair, like an attorney laying her case to rest.

"I think I see. So it's the belief in curses that causes the run of bad luck or misfortune, right?" Jason said, smiling. He looked down at the clipboard, then back up at her.

"Right." Lilly replied. That uneasy feeling returned. She shivered a tiny bit in an effort to shake it off.

"And curses are not real?" Jason said, like a good investigative reporter. He leaned the clipboard against the arm of the chair, on the inside, next to him and turned his attention back on her.

"Nope. Not in the least," Lily said, earnestly, "the *belief* in them is very real. But the curses themselves are not." Lily crossed her legs again, left over right, leaned back in her chair, and took a sip of her tea. It was cold, but she held onto the cup.

Jason leaned back in his chair. "What about all the people out there who say evil covens or "cults" have brainwashed them into doing something against their will?" He smiled at the camera. "They crop up in the news from time to time. Some of them are even quite famous."

Lilly sighed. "They do and it's rubbish. It's impossible to make someone do anything against their will unless you overpower them physically or have some other hold over them. You can't just brainwash someone and make them do anything against their will. There are always other factors involved." She leaned forward. "Don't get me wrong. There are times when it can happen but those are very difficult to accomplish. Most people will change a behavior to please someone else, but they will always revert back to their old ways. It is inevitable. You have to mentally overpower them and change their behavior patterns before a negative suggestion can even take effect. It takes a lot of effort to brainwash someone successfully – years even." Backing off a little, she sat back in her chair but felt unsettled. "There has been instances where that has happened but they are almost always extreme cases, not ordinary circumstances. The *Manchurian Candidate* movie is a good example - but, on the other hand, it's a MOVIE and not reality."

"What about voodoo and other forms of bewitchment?" Jason asked. A red light flashed in the corner as someone darted out of the control booth. He ignored it, his entire attention on her.

Lily caught the flash of the lights from that room before her eyes darted to Randy. He smiled at her. Her heart leaped and she wrenched her attention back to Jason. "If you look at all of the different philosophies out there, you'll find an underlying belief system in play for each of them. That belief system is the entire key; I cannot stress this hard enough. If you don't believe wholeheartedly that something like that can harm you, it will have no effect on you. Period." Lilly said. "Even if you believe in it just a little bit as a concept, you have to believe that *the curse will work on you before it will*. It's not enough to just know it's there, you have to believe it can actually harm you. And in effect, you are allowing it to control you. By that time and under those circumstances, you are harming yourself and the curse is a byproduct now."

"Byproduct? What makes you so sure?" Jason said, smirking. He glanced at his clipboard and said, "Isn't it just possible that someone can control your life without you knowing about it?"

"No. I've studied human behavior since I was a small child, and I know how humans behave. I've studied religion, all different forms, for clues to how humans relate to outside stimuli. I'm a certified hypnotherapist now, and the entire reason I became one is to test my theories," Lilly said. She set her cup back on the table and "That's why it's impossible to make someone do something against their will. The entire key to someone controlling your life is that you have to allow them to do so, and that's across the board. I find it utterly fascinating."

"Why would someone claim they'd been bewitched?" Jason asked, leaning forward. "I mean," he waved his hand in front of him, palm up, as if to encompass the whole room, "given that you are saying it's not possible for them to be."

Lilly refolded her hands in her lap. "There are three reasons that pop into my head why someone could claim that and make it believable, other than a cry for attention. Number one is that people are genuinely gullible. They believe anything if you explain it in words they understand. Number two is that belief system we spoke of before has been in force for generations. But even that belief system means nothing without the third reason - and that is finding someone open to your suggestions. Without all three of these reasons, magic would die almost immediately."

"Uh huh." Jason said. His entire manner dripped skepticism. He sat back in his chair, slumped sideways, leaned on one arm of his chair, and propped his head up with a fist under his chin.

"It's true. All you have to do is look at religion objectively, and you'll see it for yourself," Lilly said earnestly. "That principle covers voodoo, witchcraft, Christianity, and any other religion you can think of."

"Do you believe in God?" Jason fired the question at her. "I do."

"Doesn't that mean you're just as gullible as the rest of us, then?"

Lilly shifted her weight on the chair. "Yes, it does, in a way. It's the nature of man to believe in something bigger and greater than himself. In that, I am no different than anyone else." She made a mental note to mention how uncomfortable the chairs were after the show.

"Well! That's certainly enlightening. That's all the time we have for the first half of the show, folks. Stay tuned for the second half of the show right after the station break. Remember to call in with your questions! Lilly will be right here with us, won't you?" Jason turned to her.

"Of course," Lilly answered. *Like I would refuse in front of hundreds of witnesses*, she thought, glancing at the camera.

"Good! See you after the break, folks!" Jason smiled at the camera until the red light went off, then turned to her. Eyeing her apprehensively, he said, "So. How are we doing over there?"

"Fine, except for these chairs. You?" Lilly smiled, shifting her weight. "It looked like I rattled your cage a few times."

"Me? Nope, not at all." Jason said, picking up a glass of water placed there by a camera aide. "I'm just ducky." He sipped the water, then put the glass back on the table. "Hey, do you really believe all that stuff you were saying?"

"Yes. I wasn't kidding, you know. I've studied people for over thirty years, Jason. I have seen the same thing over and over again. I don't doubt my theory at all." Lilly said, wiping her sweaty hands on her skirt. She looked at them, puzzled. That had certainly never happened before. She saw that the camera aide had given her a glass of water, too. The surface of the water sparkled in the light from the spotlights like sunlight on the surface of a lake.

"Well, be prepared, then. My viewers love to challenge theories. The lines are probably lit up already." Jason looked over at the sound booth. "Ah, yes. I see they are."

Lilly laughed, and wondered what Maggie was doing.

Maggie took the opportunity the station break offered and used it to retrieve her makeup case from the bathroom. Taking a few minutes, she stood before the full-length bathroom mirror, and admired her reflection. A tall girl with short, raven black hair and electric blue eyes stared back at her. She turned sideways, scanning her figure. She ran long fingers over her flat belly, following the curves of her waist upwards to her full breasts. Striking a beefcake pose, she tossed her hair back and laughed. Perfect white teeth grinned at her from the mirror.

"Not bad," she said to herself. Her eyes fell on the clock, and she hurriedly pulled on matching black satin underwear. She grabbed her makeup case and a mirror, then hesitated. At the last second, she tossed a long silky transparent black blouse over her arm, in case Zeke showed up early, and streaked into the living room with her booty just as the program came back on.

"Welcome back, folks! You are watching "Topics for the New Millennium" with me, your host, Jason Dooley. Our guest today is Lillian Wassanbloom, a local psychic, otherwise known as Madame Selena." Jason smiled and gestured towards Lilly. Lilly smiled at the camera, and Jason said, "Ok. I can see the lines lit up, so let's take a caller." Jason watched the cameraman. When he pointed at him, Jason said, "Hello! You are on the air!"

"Hello?" a soft pitched female voice said. A high voice, it echoed off the walls of the room.

"Hi, caller! Do you have a question?" Jason asked, grinning at the camera. He picked up his water.

"I do. Earlier you were talking about religions and beliefs being the key to work successful magic. Would that go for other countries as well or is it just for here?" The voice sounded genuinely curious.

Jason turned to Lilly. "I believe this one is for you." He giggled at his own joke.

Lilly looked at the camera. "That concept would apply to any country that has a religious network, caller. What did you say your name was?"

"I didn't. Thanks." The caller hung up.

Jason said immediately, "Thanks for calling, whoever you were. Let's take another call."

"Hello?" a male voice, deep, said nervously.

"Go ahead, caller, you're on the air." Jason answered.

"Hi. My name is Mike, and I have a question for Lilly."

"Go ahead, Mike. I'm listening." Lilly looked at the camera and smiled.

"Yeah. I've been studying voodooism for a couple of years now, and I found out some interesting stuff. Take the practice of hanging a white rooster upside down on someone's front door. That symbolizes that a curse has been enacted on someone in the house, right?" Mike said, his voice getting faster as he talked.

"Right," Lilly agreed. "That is what it means generally."

"Well, how do the inhabitants know who the curse is for? I've found no documentation that says they put a name tag on the chicken, nor otherwise indicate who it is intended for." Mike said seriously.

Lilly looked at Jason, who looked back at her as if to say, 'it's your ball.' She looked back at the camera. "Mike, to tell you the truth, it would depend on who was in the house and what they had been doing lately."

She wiped her palms again. "See, the chicken is a symbol that everyone in that community would recognize, right? So that would mean that whoever in the house that's hiding something would react most violently to the stimulus, and there you have it. Does that help you?"

"It does. Thanks, Lilly." Mike hung up. The studio buzzed with empty air, then the connection was broken.

"Take a minute and explain that one a bit more, Lilly. It's got me stumped, and I'm sure I'm not the only one," Jason said, nodding at the camera.

"No problem. Okay. In said community, the chicken would symbolize a curse has been enacted, right?" Lilly said. Jason nodded, and she continued. "It's an easily recognized symbol that everyone understands. You hang that symbol on someone's door, everybody recognizes it, and everyone believes its true. Someone within is going to react to it, and that someone is whoever has done something considered wrong or sinful by themselves or others. Therefore, this person takes on the responsibility of the curse, and it comes to pass. The truth of the entire matter is that someone's belief has brought a suggestion to reality." Lilly smiled. "Got it?"

"Yes," Jason said, nodding. "Let's take another caller." He listened for the 'click', then said, "Hello! Welcome to 'Topics For The New Millennium.' You're on the air."

"Thank you, Jason. Would you ask Lilly is she believes in the devil, or demons incarnate?" A female voice said. A note of triumph sounded through the room.

"You could ask her yourself, caller. She's right here." Jason said, smiling at Lilly.

"But it's your show, Jason. I've been listening to her flap her beak for 45 minutes. I watch the show because of you, not her." The caller said, her voice vicious. The cameramen shifted their position as if to rush to Lilly's aid, but they stayed put.

"I appreciate that, caller. What did you say your name was?" Jason asked, staring up at the speaker in the ceiling. The camera panned to Lilly, catching the look on her face perfectly.

Lilly stared at Jason, dumbstruck. Had she been monopolizing the show? She didn't think so. Jason had guided the conversation, and wasn't that what guests were supposed to do? Share their knowledge with the audience? Hastily, she brought her attention back to the caller.

"Iris Dean. I'm from Mirror Lake." The caller said.

Lilly shivered, and wiped her palms again. There was something about that voice that bothered her. She glanced at Randy. He was staring up at the speaker overhead, a frozen look of horror on his face. She was staring at him, puzzled, when Iris' voice dragged her attention back to the studio.

"Are you saying you know Lilly?" Jason asked. He raised his eyebrows at Lilly.

"Most assuredly I know her. But she doesn't know me yet." Iris said, a note of glee in her voice. "I've been following her for years."

The last word echoed in Lilly's head, like an echo following a mountain chain, each repeat lower in volume. Lilly had the impression of a tall, dark, shadowy figure stalking her, darting out of sight just as she turned, drawing a bead on her when she wasn't looking. She blanched, and put a hand up to her chest. Immediately, she felt vulnerable to the fates, like the Gods were watching from Olympus. Her skin prickled in a cold sweat. She could feel her own heart beating against her breastbone like a wild animal trapped in a cage.

Jason looked at her, then up at the speakers. The cameraman snapped his fingers, and when Jason looked at him, pointed to the camera lens. "How do you know her?" Jason asked, staring into the camera.

"She's my twin sister, that's how," Iris stated.

Lilly's eyes rolled back in her head. Her hands shot forward, gripping the chair arms on either side and her knuckles white. Her eyes refocused, and she stared malevolently at the camera. In a deep voice, not her own, she rasped, "War is coming, BEWARE! The fate of mankind hangs on the outcome. All who hear this have one task - pray for the good side to win. The evil one is strong now." Lilly's eyes bored into the camera for a few more seconds, then she pointed at it and screamed "Beware!" Her eyes rolled back in her head, and she jerked out of the chair and landed face down on the floor, her feet towards the camera. Her body lay still as if dead.

Low, evil chuckling came from the speakers overhead as Jason gestured frantically for a commercial break. "Folks, we will return shortly." He gestured, and said, "Go to a commercial! For God's sake, go to a commercial!" The camera cut off as Jason bent down to administer aide to Lilly.

Maggie stared at the TV, dumbstruck, a mascara applicator brush raised halfway to her face. One eye was already outlined heavily, gothic-style, in mascara and black eyeliner. "Impossible," she said out loud, although there was nobody else there. "Mom's an only child."

The doorbell rang, and Maggie shoved the applicator brush back in the tube of mascara. Tossing it on the table with the rest of her makeup, she threw the transparent blouse on, and unaware of the striking figure she posed, she hurried to the front door and threw it open.

Zeke dropped his hand and threw his cigarette off the side of the porch into the bushes. Running his fingers through his tufty brownish-black hair, he said, "Well, I see you're not ready yet." He looked to the left and the right, then back at her. His eyes traveled down then back up again. "It's a good damn thing you don't have neighbors, or I'd have a whole lot to say about what you're not wearing, too."

Mirror Lake, Montana, was a very small, tree-fraught community in the middle of the state, located down the mountain from the lake with the same name. There was a flat surface at the foot of the mountain, and that is where the original inhabitants settled in the early 1900's. By the time Fred Wilder and his group showed up, the town was already established. In Maggie's day, the town had about 500 residents, including her and her mother. The main street had a small local fruit market, mostly filled with produce from the neighboring farms, and a gas station where you could rent movies as well as buy gas. The day the Slushie machine arrived half the town showed up to watch. The town also had a florist shop, a thrift store, a police station, and a place to buy ice cream. All the shops were on one side of the street facing a mountain. The houses where people lived were on the other side of the mountain. Most properties were at least five miles out of town. People had house trailers nestled amongst the trees on their properties with long winding driveways leading to them. Regular runs to Virginia City to get those things not available in Mirror Lake were common, and the school buses came from there too.

Maggie's house sat at the end of a long driveway on the south end of Mirror Lake. There were no neighbors close by, just trees and bushes. She shrugged. "I need a few more minutes, is all." She stepped away from the door, letting him in. "I'm watching Mom on TV. Want to come in and wait?"

Zeke shrugged back. "I suppose. Beats cooling my heels out here." He entered the house and said, "Oh, yeah. She had that talk show today." He entered the foyer, following Maggie, seeing the little mosaic-tiled table on the left as if for the first time. He loved the wooden frame on it, and thought the little drawer in the front was nicely done, and he even admired the ringed pull on it. Walking up the hallway, he sauntered past open French doors into the living room. The doors opened towards each side like flower petals, and were filled with clear glass panels. Intricate patterns of leading etched out roses and lilies across the surface of both doors. Zeke loved those doors. He thought they were gorgeous. He ran his fingers along the piping every time he went in and out of that room, careful not to smudge the glass. The walls had old-fashioned plum colored wallpaper with grape clusters here and there placed on it. The huge windows stretched from floor to ceiling and were four times as wide as normal windows, and had purple curtains gathered and draped dramatically off to the sides. Crown molding ringed the ceilings. In front of one of the windows was a lounger, pillows strewn across it, and a plush, light brown throw laying across the head, as if waiting for someone to return to it.

A big flat screen TV sat against the back wall, to the right when you walked into the room, with a dark brown suede sectional couch facing the TV. A coffee table lay between the couch and the TV, with 2 comfortable overstuffed brown-suede chairs facing the coffee table. A throw rug lay under the furniture, light brown in color, over a darker brown plush carpet. Various smaller pieces dotted the room as decor, and in other places house plants spread their branches and bloomed all over the house. Every room had plants in it.

Past the front room was the parlor with another set of inside ornate doors, this time decorated with roses alone. Walking into the room felt light and breezy. The furniture within was antique. Chairs had high backs with wooden frames curving along the top and gracefully sloping down the sides into ornately carved chair arms. Sturdy wooden frames pillowed pure white upholstery decorated with lilacs in bloom in clusters here and there on the surface. Clawed feet completed the chairs. Another coffee table was in this room. Diaphanous white curtains hung in the room and fluttered in the breeze, giving the entire room a light airy smell. Along the wall opposite the door was a huge natural wood fireplace.

The hallway continued, wrapping around the interior of the first floor, leading the way to different rooms. Across from the parlor, on the right side of the hall was a door to a small storage room under the stairs. This room was not decorated at all. Wooden shelves lining the walls were for placing things on. The lower shelf was double high for storage bins and other oversized items. The entire room was lit by bare hanging bulbs from the ceiling. Another small table sat against the wall on the right, before you got to the door to the room. The kitchen was in the back of the house, and it was a wonder to behold. Every modern convenience was in that kitchen.

Walking in, the fridge was on the left side of the room. A short counter space (originally intended for food prep) separated the fridge and the huge industrial stove. The stove had six burners, two ovens side by side, and a storage shelf a little higher than eye level for cooking paraphernalia. Cupboards ringed the walls both above and below the counter. A huge double sink with a Moen "Touchie" faucet that had a spray attachment included sat in the middle under a window that looked out over the back yard. An island with another stove in the counter top lay in the middle of the kitchen. Dark wood paneling matched the shade of the cupboards, and the granite top was green-flecked gold. A egg-shell white tiled floor completed the look.

Off the kitchen, in the back corner, was the laundry room. This had a state of the art front loading washer and dryer, maroon, and a table for folding and sorting. Laundry supplies were kept in a cupboard out of sight. An ironing board hung on the wall behind the door, with an iron resting in a holder above it. The floor was light green flecked linoleum.

Opposite corner on the back of the house was the dining room. The room had an Oak table in the middle that sat a dozen people, and there were matching upholstered chairs around it. The chairs were wooden framed (Oak) with that deep rich honey brown color, with gold upholstery on the seats and backs. Most of the time the table was set too, as if waiting for dinner guests. A dark brown buffet cabinet sat off to the side on the right side, each drawer with ringed pulls on them. A China cabinet on the left side of the room displayed fine China plates in holders with delicate China teacups in saucers in front of each. The floor in this room was off white plush carpet. This room was seldom used.

Smack in the middle of the first floor was a stairway directly opposite the front door. Upon walking into the house you could go to the left towards the Front Room, up the stairs to the second floor, or off to the right, which was where the Reading Room and the Office/Library was.

The Reading Room was where Lilly worked at home. Most of her clients came to her, and she did whatever they needed within that space. She offered Tarot Readings, Palmistry, Hypnosis Sessions, and general Spiritual Counseling sessions. Her reading room had a small lace-draped table in the middle with two comfortable, matching, maroon-upholstered Captain's chairs for Tarot (chairs set so the door was on the Lilly's left and neither her nor the client faced the door nor had their back to it, Lilly also sat facing West) a comfortable overstuffed light green corduroy lounge chair for Hypnosis, a comfortable light green corduroy couch for that same purpose, and a plain white double-doored cupboard for supplies so they were not on display during readings. Extra stuff not intended for the current reading taking place were considered distractions, and she put them away if they were not needed. This storage cupboard was also where she kept her stones and crystals and her cleansing tools for when she did blessings or cleaned haunted houses. A painted lavender bearded iris graced the front of the cupboard, it's petals outlined with a fine toothed brush to bring out the details.

The office/library was standard. Walking into it was like walking onto a different planet. A large wooden desk sat out from the back wall, facing the interior of the house with it's back towards an enormous window facing west. The setting sun lit up the entire room with blazing colors. Lilly loved to work in that office. This was where she officially worked and studied her projects. A computer sat on her desk, on the left so it didn't obstruct her view of the door. Along the left wall, while sitting at the desk, was a line of filing cabinets. Client's files, research notes, everything she accumulated was kept in those cabinets. A television faced the desk with a comfortable light red loveseat in between, facing the TV. This was for viewing videos etcetera. This room had light green short-plush carpet. Along all the walls that didn't have something against it were bookshelves stocked full of books on all kinds of subjects.

FEDEX knew exactly where they lived.

Maggie led the way to the living room. Zeke followed. She sat back on the couch and picked up the mascara again. She pulled the brush out and patted the couch cushion next to her. "Come on, you gotta see this. Mom just fainted." Picking up the hand mirror, she checked the one eye to make sure it still looked good and prepared to mascara the other eye.

Zeke sat next to her. The coffee table was full of makeup-smeared tissues, as well as the contents of Maggie's makeup case. They made him feel funny, like he had invaded someone's turf. He flexed his muscles. "How come you're not worried?"

Maggie rubbed the applicator brush against her eyelashes, watching in the mirror and comparing eyes to make sure they matched. "What makes you think I'm not?" She replaced the applicator brush and picked up the eyeliner.

Zeke put a hand on her thigh, and she froze. He squeezed, feeling the firm warm flesh beneath his hand. "You don't look worried."

She looked at his hand, then back up to his face just as the program came on again. He grinned at her, not leering but as if to say *it's ok, I'm here now*. Maggie glanced at the screen; Lilly was once again sitting at the counter, and Jason was talking. She was a bit pale but otherwise didn't look that much different than she did earlier in the program. She flicked her eyes back to Zeke. *He has the bluest eyes*, she thought. Out loud, she said, "I knew she'd be ok, see?" She pointed to the TV as if that was all the proof she needed.

"Uh huh," Zeke said, not looking. He squeezed again. "Seeing that she's not home..."

Maggie went back to her eyeliner and her mirror. Her thigh felt like it was on fire; she could feel his pulse through her skin. Nonchalantly, she said, "We'd end up being late."

Zeke took his hand off her leg and rubbed it on his own jean-clad thigh, not like he was trying to wipe her off his hand but as if to join the two together. "We could always go to later show."

Maggie applied some black lipstick. "Yeah. Then I could be late for curfew." She horsed into the mirror, checking her teeth for black lipstick.

"Alright, alright! Forget I brought it up." Zeke said, exasperated, his voice a touch deeper. He picked up one of the tissues off the table and began to shred it. "I'm not interested in your body anyhow." Little flecks of shredded tissue wafted down around him like a ticker tape parade.

Maggie laughed. "Liar." Standing up, she wrapped the blouse around her like she could hide her shape in it and faced him. "Zeke, you know there's a time and a place for everything."

"I thought there was always time for *that*," Zeke said, his eyes raking her figure. He licked his lips. "Oh, my."

Maggie smiled. "I'm gonna finish getting dressed, then we can go, ok?" She walked out of the room, knowing that his eyes followed her. It was always like that. They often shared the same thoughts and feelings, and they each thought of themselves as a perfect match. She knew most of the time what he was thinking, and she knew he did too. Theirs was a very close and intimate bond, and one she cherished.

He shouted after her, "Someday you're going to want me as much as I want you, you know!" Irritably, he lit a cigarette, and threw one leg over the other. Laying back against the couch, he slouched and blew smoke at the ceiling.

She shouted back, "I know!" A few seconds later, she shouted, "And don't smoke in the house! Mom will have a cow!"

Zeke rolled his eyes and continued puffing on the cigarette, but carefully didn't move. He'd never seen anyone have a cow before; it might just be worth watching.

Iris Dean hung up the phone, a smirk of satisfaction on her face. The smirk quickly faded as her thoughts turned to her sister. She flicked some papers on her desk, staring thoughtfully at the bookshelves across the room. Her desk was Oak, huge and heavy with large clawed feet. The desk surface was 6 feet long and 5 feet wide, and shone in the fading daylight as if oiled. Oak book shelves lined the same wall that held the only door to the room. The door was also Oak, engraved and thick with an old-fashioned pearl doorknob. An ancient Oak staff, about 8 feet tall and laden with charms and pendants leaned against the bookshelves close to the door, as if protecting the room. It had belonged to other High Priests of the Coven, and rested in a place of honor in her office. She believed in it's power. Iris had a Silver Dragon's Head knocker installed on the outside of the door, and required all who wished to enter to knock. Huge glass panes formed the back wall of the office, showing the woods as a background for the room. Iris loved her living mural. It was better than any paint job she could have asked for.

Dark blue plush carpet graced the floor, the large heavy desk faced the inside of the room. About five feet into the room from the front of the desk was a large circle in the floor. The slab was a black marble circle with a gold pentagram etched in the center. The carpet did not encroach on the marble.

Walking to the middle of the room, she stopped smack in the middle of the pentagram, and faced the glass wall. Raising her arms up to the ceiling in a worshipful gesture, she intoned, "Thank you, Hakon!" Dropping her arms, she held her hands together in front of her chest, reverently, saying again, "Thank you."

Walking out of the pentagram, she crossed to her altar in the corner of the room to the left of the door. There was no floor. The barn floor opened and met bare ground in this corner, with a wooden barrier separating the woods from civilization and ringing a tree stump. This tree stump stood about four feet high and was covered in bark. It had been sawed off to make a flat table surface, and was four feet wide in all directions. The trunk had been hallowed out and fitted with a door that opened to reveal a hiding place within the tree, where most of the paraphernalia for Iris' personal religious services were stored.

Iris ran her hands over the bark covered stump, she closed her eyes and reaffirmed her ties with it as a holy item. Kissing the top, she lit a match and lit the four candles on the stump, starting from the left. All four candles were black. Lighting an incense cone, she placed it in a dragon-shaped holder, and waited until the smoke started to waft out of the nostrils. Passing her hands through it, she directed its rise toward the ceiling, saying, "Accept this smoke as a gift, Hakon."

Bowing to the altar, Iris crossed the room to her desk. Eyeing the altar with satisfaction, she tapped the space bar on her laptop, reactivating it. Her desktop wallpaper popped into view, a picture of Beltane dancers swirling around a bonfire by the light of a full moon, and she smiled. Clicking on her log, she waited till the program came up and started to type:

> *Today I contacted Lilly by phone while she was guesting on a television program. You remember Lilly, right? I've told you about her before. Hakon mentioned her when I was a child, but I forgot about her until recently. I'm still a touch surprised to find confirmation about her after all these years; after all, I thought I was an only child. Good thing David found that old logbook from 37 years ago, or we'd never would have known what happened to her.*
>
> *I wish I could use her for the ritual, but it's almost ludicrous to assume she's still a virgin. Actually, you know I've always lusted after that position myself, but even though I am still pure, I cannot preside over the ritual and participate in it too. Hakon insists his priestess remain pure! So, we'll have to investigate Lilly. You know we must have a virgin or the ritual will be all in vain. After all, that's what was wrong 37 years ago. I'm glad Lachlan roasts in hell for all eternity.*
>
> *Anyway, thanks to him, our mother was not a virgin. We were born, both human and powerless. Note to self: Check out possibility of using Lillian for ritual anyway...demon blood has to count for something, doesn't it? Ah, yes, we have to definitely begin investigating Lilly and her life. There may be something we can use her for. Like I said, pity I can't use myself. I'd love the prestige!*

Iris continued to type for about 10 minutes, then punched the intercom on her desk. "David, come in here please." She continued to type until a tall, brown-haired man came in.

"You wanted to see me?" David White said, his baritone voice resonant. He was 6'3", wide-shouldered and barrel chested, with narrow hips. His biceps bulged under his black robe. A long, tasseled hood hung down the back. When worn, the hood hid his entire face. His brown eyes flicked around the room, he noticed the candles on her altar, and smiled, totally changing his looks. "You made contact?"

"Of course. The silly fool fainted on the air." Iris said, an evil grin on her face. Her short blond hair was barely long enough to ripple in the breeze from the window. That same breeze blew her robes up into her lap, exposing her long legs. She brushed them back down. Fixing him with her black eyes, she said, "I need you to start investigating her, Jinx. Since I can't use myself for the ritual, maybe we can use her."

"Indeed." David raised his eyebrows. "Why can't we use you? You're still a virgin, right?" He glanced at the altar, then back to her. "You know it's ridiculous to assume she's still a virgin."

Iris shot a disdainful look at him and picked up a pile of papers from the shelf behind her desk. "That may be true. You know I am still pure, but I can't very well preside over the ritual and star in it too." She irritably slammed the papers on the desk in front of her.

"You can if you let me preside." David said, his tone exasperated, as if it was a recurring discussion. He resented the fact that she made him stand in front of the desk instead of letting him sit, like a little kid seeing the principal. He had even said so to the few he felt were loyal to him within the coven. He was careful to not make too loud of a noise, though. One had to tread carefully when plotting treachery.

"You know I can't do that, although I would love too. Hakon only speaks to me," Iris said, matter-of-factly. "I am tired of discussing this. Every time we speak of the ritual, you want to know why you can't preside over it. Your place in the Ill Wind Coven is master-at-arms. This you know, Jinx. You are the peacemaker, and the peacekeeper, plus you are the investigative arm we need." She shut her laptop, leaving it on. "Stop bringing it up."

"Sorry." David said, his tone still angry. "Everybody has ambitions, Acantha. You can't fault me for that." He flicked his robe against his leg slightly. It was the only sign of his discontent.

"Nor do I. There's just no place for it right now." Iris got up, and crossed over to him. Standing directly in front of him, she placed a hand gently on the inside of his arm against the crook of his elbow and looked up into his face, almost like a lover would, and said, "I can't promise anything, but we'll keep it in mind, ok?"

"Like an escape plan?" David asked, hopefully, looking down into her face. Catching himself staring at her lips, his eyes rose to meet hers. Seeing the smirk in her eyes, he swallowed nervously then straightened like a man not ashamed to be attracted to her.

"Yes. If we get desperate." Iris dropped her hand from his arm. "Now, go. Do as I command."

"Yes, High Priestess." David bowed and left. The door politely slammed behind him with a solid 'thud'.

Iris watched him go and sighed. Sometimes the fact that Hakon demanded his high priestess be a virgin was hard to live with.

"There's been contact, Bart," Randy said later that evening. He'd seen Lilly home and to bed, staying with her until she'd fallen asleep. That was upstairs. He was now calling his leader on her house phone downstairs in the living room.

"You are calling from her place?" Bart asked, his deep voice unmistakable.

Randy could just about see Bart in his mind's eye. A huge black man, with short close-cropped hair, deep brown eyes and a kindly face. Basically a bodybuilder type, although Bart was not one to go to a gym. He came by it naturally, the lucky dog. Randy said, "Yeah. Lilly's asleep, and Maggie's still out on her date."

"Ok, then. So what happened?"

Randy sighed. "Iris called her during the second half of the show, and dropped the shoe. Iris told her they were twins." Randy sat forward, picking up one of Maggie's tissues and playing with it. He didn't notice it smudged his fingers with makeup. "Were you watching?" Randy looked to the TV as if to see if Lilly had appeared on it, but the big flat screen showed a dark face.

"No. I had a crisis to handle." Bart said, his tone one of regret. "I should have set a timer for it. I was afraid of something like that. I had a feeling about it. Maybe I can get a copy of the transcript or the tape for tonight's show and see it myself."

"Good idea on getting the tape. Even if you had said something it wouldn't have changed tonight's events. Anyhow, Lilly spazzed out. She got all raspy and started talking about a coming war between good and evil." Randy said, sitting back on the couch.

"Did the voice recommend a strategy?" Bart asked, excitedly.

"It said to pray for the good side to win." Randy said. "Why?"

"That's all she said?"

"Basically, yeah. Then she fainted right there on camera," Randy said. "I didn't expect that."

"Don't know anybody who does," Bart said. "I don't think she did either." He chuckled, low in his throat, but not unkindly.

"She's exhausted at the moment. Fell out as soon as we got here." Randy looked up at the ceiling towards the bedroom where Lilly was sleeping. "I'm just gonna wait here until Maggie gets home so she won't be alone."

"Good idea. Keep me posted." Bart cleared his throat. "And don't obsess about it. Channeling often wears out the receiver." He hung up.

Randy looked at the dead telephone in his hand. "You could have mentioned that before now, too, Bart." He hung up the phone, and turned on the TV. He had at least an hour before Maggie was supposed to be back. He might as well make himself to home.

CHAPTER TWO

Bart Jackson hung up the phone, already brooding about the conversation and the things Randy had said. This was bad. Iris was well known for her impetuousness; leave it to her to jump the gun and ruin everything. Drat it. He'd have to set the watch on Lilly and Maggie sooner than expected. He punched the intercom button on his desk. "Ted?"

"Yes?" Theodore Davis answered, his baritone voice drifting through the desk unit. The off white speaker sat on a mahogany desk. A desk calendar lay on the desktop directly in front of Bart, some dates crossed off with a black X. An open laptop was positioned for his right hand, the phone on the left of the huge desk. An old-fashioned Rolodex was on display, to the right of the phone but not quite in the middle of the front of the desk (which means whomever was sitting facing him wouldn't have a Rolodex in their view) along with a matching desk lamp on the corner behind the laptop and a metal pencil holder out in front. Other than these few items, the desktop was bare and highly polished.

Bart cleared his throat and said into the unit, "Come in here a moment, will you?"

"Sure." An audible 'click' and the office door opened almost immediately. A tall man came in, his rusty red hair close cropped and his brown eyes full of curiosity. He looked comfortable in a periwinkle blue pullover and loose fitting jeans. White tennis shoes completed the ensemble. "What's up, Bart? You almost never ask me to come inside." He carried a steno pad and a pen.

"I need you to do something. I need you to locate Honey and Nicholas for me. I've got jobs for them." Bart smiled slightly, as if he was chipping away at the panic he could hear in himself.

Ted opened his steno pad, and started writing furiously. "Any particular time you need them to be here? And do they need to bring anything?"

"As soon as possible and nothing is required other than their presence. Their task is important." Bart lifted his talisman to his lips and kissed it, closing his eyes as if in reverent prayer. Opening them again, he said. "It's starting, Ted, just like we knew it would." He hoped the look of disbelief and panic he saw on Ted's face wasn't mirrored on his own.

Ted stared at Bart, his eyes wide. "Really. The timing could have been better, but that figures, doesn't it?" He flipped the notebook closed and clipped his pen to his shirtfront where the neckline parted. The clicker hung there, a splash of red against the blue like a streak of blood. Bart sent another prayer up as the red pen took on a "glow" - the aura he could see around objects when they bespoke an event or were an omen of upcoming disaster - and he hoped it didn't herald Ted's demise in the coming battle. Ted was one of his best buddies, and besides, good help was hard to find.

"Yes," Bart agreed. "We don't have a lot of time, Ted. The ritual is imminent, and we have to do what we can to stop it." He sighed heavily.

"Right. I'll find Honey and Nick as soon as possible and send them around. Anything else?" Ted said. The pen still had an aura, but it was a little less than before. The aura was fading and that was a good sign.

Bart felt his hopes rise a smidgen. "Nope. Not at the moment."

"Alrighty, then." Ted stopped on his way to the door. "You all set in here? Need anything to drink or whatever?"

"I'm fine. Oh, do you think you can call the television station and get a copy of tonight's 'Topics for the New Millennium' show? It has a record of the initial contact between the twins." Bart said, lowering his gaze to the floor, where papers piled up on both sides of him. Each pile represented some project under development. "And make a note to remind me to organize my papers, will ya?"

"Yes, sir!" Ted said, grinning. "I'll make it top priority." He wrote while he spoke, "Remind Bart to peddle his papers." He laughed and left the room.

"You do that." Shaking his head, he watched Ted leave. Even the camaraderie between him and Ted didn't really dispel the gloom and doom he felt. This was going to be a bad scene, he thought. Never had the responsibility of his station in the Bright Star coven weigh so heavily on him as it did now.

Brooding, he stared at his bookcase, and the books within. Getting up, he crossed the light brown shag carpet to the mahogany bookcases, three in all lining a wall in his office, and pulled out an oversized red velvet-clad book from the middle bookcase. Cradling it lovingly in his arms, he carried it carefully to the desk and laid it reverently on the desktop.

He ran his hands across the jacket, allowing the velvet to pick up his energy. He opened it, and carefully flipped the pages until he found the page he was looking for.

Opening his desk, he pulled out a pad and a pen, and prepared to take notes. "Page one," he said to himself, reading from the book. "The first thing you must have to prevent a demon raising is a coven at full strength. Only the combined good will of a full coven can start the expulsion process..." Bart began to write, making a mental note that the first requirement was already met. He worked on his notes for a while, then clicked the light out. Thinking for a short while, he mulled over the beginning of a plan then went to bed.

Jenny Walker stood about 5'3" in her stocking feet, and had dark strawberry blonde hair cut short. She was pear-shaped with a beautiful smile and blue-green eyes. She was the manager and owner of the local Flower Shoppe, and she was supposed to accept a delivery early that day, before the shop opened for business. She arrived to find the deliveryman already there, lounging against his truck. "You're early," she said, snicking the key in the lock and opening the door.

"The curse of the working man," he drawled. He was skinny, with a pockmarked face and stringy, greasy black hair. He opened the spring-released latch on the truck's back door, and pushed it up. Boxes lined the insides of the truck. He waved at a dozen boxes closest to him. "Where do you want them?"

"Inside." Jenny turned the key in the storage room door. "Just put them here until I can check the shipping receipt."

The man mumbled to himself as he lugged the boxes in. Jenny listened to him tell himself that today was gonna be one of THOSE days from the front of the store, smirking as she started the coffee machine. A 'bang' brought her running to the back room.

"What was that?" Jenny said, alarmed. She looked around for the disaster, but nothing looked out of place. A large green table stretched across the back of the work room, various containers on it sporting the tools of the trade. This particular table was used for arrangements, and had, among other things, a large roller on the one end for paper and another directly behind it loaded with clear cellophane. The corkboard wall behind the table sported pliers (short and long-nosed), wirecutters, channel locks, lengths of wire, and twist-ties, and various kinds of tape suspended from hooks just waiting to be grabbed. Empty vases dotted the surface here and there. Spots on the table of glue, glitter, and other things attested to it's daily use.

"I'm done," the deliveryman said, slapping the nearest box. The pile compressed a bit from the impact, and expanded again almost immediately. He pulled a clipboard off the top and handed it to her. "Just sign here."

She looked over the manifest. Roses. Opening the nearest box, Jenny picked up one of the flowers. The rose petals flaked off and drifted to the floor, leaving only the stamen. Other boxes revealed the same malady, but not all of them. She carried the clipboard out of the storage room, slapping it against her jeans, a slight frown on her face.

The deliveryman had watched her inspect the boxes, his face turning more and more sour with each one. After the third box, he shook his own head and mumbled even more often and a little bit louder about the day not being what he expected. When she walked out of the work room carrying the clipboard, he followed her.

"I've got a problem," she said to him. "Half the roses you brought me are frost bitten. The petals are going to fall off before I can even get them out of the boxes." She lay the clipboard on the counter and leaned on it, facing him. Not that she wanted to. He was not even the least bit attractive to her.

The deliveryman's eyes narrowed. "At least they got here." He crossed his arms over his chest and flipped his hair out of his face. It was so greasy it stuck in the flipped back position for a second or two before it lazily drifted back up over his head to get in his face again.

"That is not the point. I can't sell them." Jenny slapped the clipboard on the counter. "What am I supposed to do with them?" She glared at him. She had to look up at him, even though he was only a few inches taller than she was. She stuck her hands on her hips and glared at him, waiting for him to say something.

"I don't know." He shrugged. His hands shook as he reached for the clipboard. "I suppose you're going to have to call the main office. I don't trouble shoot or solve problems. I am just the delivery boy."

"I'll just do that." Jenny picked up the phone, wrapping the cord around her fingers. Her eyes darted around the interior of the flower shop. Refrigerated display cases of flowers lined the walls, decorative fronds stuck out of vases in the middle of the room. Baby's breath, peacock feathers, ivy leaves and other plants used to spice up a bouquet lay on shelving just to the left of the counter. The deliveryman was the only one in the store besides herself, and she spent every effort to avoid looking at him.

The deliveryman picked up the clipboard and examined the manifest. "Hey! You didn't sign this." He stuck a pen up under the clip and shoved it at her. His jaw jutted out belligerently. It was obvious he wanted her to sign it.

"I'm not going to sign it until I talk to someone about the damaged goods you delivered." Jenny said, trying to not listen to him as he whined about his papers while the automated attendant was giving her instructions at the same time. She punched a button on the phone. "You're just gonna have to wait."

"Aw, come on, lady. I've got other deliveries to make, you know." He shoved the clipboard closer to her. "Just sign it now, and work out the details when you get the boss on the phone."

"No. If I sign it, I accept responsibility for payment, and I'm not paying for dead flowers." Jenny turned her back on him, and scowled at the counter behind the cash register. Her fingers continued to twist the phone cord. *Honestly, the delivery people this firm hired*, she thought. *I really ought to find another supplier.*

The deliveryman slouched against the counter, hands pinned under his arms while he waited. He kept glancing at the clipboard as if expecting to find she had signed the manifest while he wasn't looking, and every time he saw it wasn't signed, he gripped his ribs tighter. He glanced at her from time to time, admiring the way her wide hips bloomed out from a tiny waist. She didn't have the greatest face, he thought, but man! What a shape from the waist down!

Jenny punched some more buttons on the phone, and finally said, "Yes, I'm calling about my delivery?" She listened for a minute, then said, "Yes, I'll hold." She continued to look at the wall instead of him.

The deliveryman drank his fill of her behind, then stared out the window, watching the town as it woke and carried on with life. Hearing a soft 'thud,' he looked in her direction. She was gone.

"Now what?" He peeked around the flowers but didn't see her. The phone was off the hook, and the cord disappeared behind the counter. His heart beat faster, and he swallowed. "Oh, lord." He found her face down on the floor behind the counter, unconscious, the phone cord still wrapped around her fingers, and the receiver in her ear screeching, "Hello? Hello? Can I help you?" Finally, the receiver clicked, and the phone died.

The deliveryman slumped to the floor in front of the counter, leaning up with his back against it, shaking violently. Now how was he going to get his signature? He contemplated things for a minute, facing the fact that this, truly, just wasn't his day. After about 10 minutes, he figured he should call somebody, and left to find a pay phone. He didn't want to touch the woman behind the counter, nor the phone she was still wearing.

Clancey's was a family-oriented restaurant on the south end of Main Street. Painted a shade of green too bright to be mistaken for foliage, the restaurant stood out like the beacon it was. Everyone went there. The place had a few different areas within for the discerning diner, ranging from a friendly drink at the bar just inside the entry to a family style, home cookin' restaurant booth seat in the back. Dark wooden ladderlike railings ringed the bar, supported by a pole here and there. The walls were a rich Asian red, as were the booths. Dark wood plating decorated the booths, ringing the upholstery like a picture frame. Small tables sat in the middle of the dining floor, each positioned so that the inhabitants felt as if they were in their own little world.

Bart looked around the restaurant he managed. Tonight was busy, apparently everyone in town had decided to go out and eat. His waitresses were frazzled, snapping at each other before picking up their orders and delivering it with the required smile to their respective customers. The low lighting tried to create an intimate atmosphere for the diners, and thankfully most of them were oblivious to the trails of waitressing.

Two of his girls had called in sick, and he was short-handed. He even ran a few orders himself, and constantly checked to make sure nobody was stiffed on good service. After all, Clancy's was known for their friendly service, good food, and reasonable prices. Why give a bad rep just because it was a bad day?

"Bart! Phone for you!" Beatrice called from the office. A small, motherly woman, she spent her breaks in the office, chain-smoking. Against the rules, but she was working a double for him, so he let that slide. She smashed out her cigarette and lit another one.

"Thanks, Bea. I'll be right there." Bart made the rounds again, finding everything ok, and sprinted for the office. Picking up the phone, he said, "Yes?" Bea left the office, pulling the door shut behind her. He pulled out a can of Lysol from a desk drawer and gave the room a spritz. He could see the kitchen area and part of the dining room by craning his neck and looking up over the partition. His office had a half wall with a picture window so he could watch the workers while in the office but he felt kinda strange sitting in the office during working hours. The waitresses were quick to take advantage of his absence, and he was too busy to iron out problems tonight. He craned his neck to check on them.

"Mr. Jackson?" a male voice said. The closed door allowed Bart to hear the voice with perfect clarity.

Bart said, "This is he. May I help you?" He waved away one of the waitresses. Every time he got on the phone…disgustedly, he slipped the can back in the desk drawer and shut it so it banged in the empty room.

"Mr. Jackson, this is Sergeant Morris at Mirror Lake PD. We need you to come down here."

"I'm sorry, but I'm working right now. Can I drop by later?" Bart fingered some papers on his desk, eyes drifting to the window across the way.

Morris huffed. "I suppose, but it's really important." Silence, the kind that got pregnant with meaning the longer it endured.

Bart felt stalked by it, and rushed to fill it. He had to get back to work, darn it. Them waitresses were slacking off, he could feel it, and said, "Well, I know it can't be family trouble, because I don't have a wife or kids. I also know it can't be that I'm in trouble with the law, because I haven't done anything wrong. Or have I?" Bart said, pointing at the orders up on the serving counter. A scrawny teenager scuttled forward, picked up the dishes, and scurried away with them.

"No, sir, nothing like that. We would like to speak to you about Jennifer Walker."

"Jenny?" Bart said, his throat closing up. "Oh, Lord. What's wrong?" He swallowed, her face springing up in his mind. "Is she ok?"

Morris' voice tightened. "I'd rather not go into it over the phone, Mr. Jackson. Can you come here right after you get off work?"

Crud. "Yes. We close in 2 hours, and I'll be there right after. Will you be there?" Bart asked, staring at the message board, but not really seeing it. "That'll be about 10 pm."

"Yep. I'll be here." Morris said, then hung up.

Bart sat heavily behind his desk. The odor of cigarette smoke still hung in the air despite the gallon of Lysol he sprayed. Hanging up the receiver, he held his head in his hands for a few minutes.

Jenny was dead. He knew it as sure as he was sitting there. He forced himself to stifle his grief and get to the business at hand. Dazed, he returned to work, not caring a fig if the last few customers were happy or not. He was accompanied by the howling of his heart, bellowing it's anguish over losing a friend.

The police station was obscenely bright for two in the morning. A streetlight aimed at the doorway like a spotlight, illuminating the way out of the darkness. Bart dragged himself in, knowing he didn't want to be there but had to go, and announced himself to the desk sergeant and seated himself in the lobby while he waited for Sergeant Morris. He used a handkerchief to wipe his eyes while a few other people in the lobby stared at him. Bart didn't care who watched.

A rather large man in a dark brown business suit entered the lobby. His hair was short and black; his intense brown eyes raked the interior. His tie and collar were loosened, tie hanging askew a bit. He immediately made a beeline for Jackson. "Mr. Bartholomew Jackson?" Morris said, extending a hand.

"Yes." Bart took the offered hand, and went to get up. "Sorry it took me so long. We were shorthanded tonight."

"No problem. Don't bother getting up, Mr. Jackson. I'm sorry to drag you here after what I'm sure was a hard day." Morris sat next to Bart, and crossed his legs. There were no others sitting nearby so the two men were like in an oasis all their own.

"Jenny's dead, isn't she?" Bart asked, his voice low and strangled.

"Yes. I'm sorry." Morris said, pulling an envelope out of his jacket and laying it across his lap. "How did you know?"

"I had a feeling. How did it happen? She was perfectly healthy the last time I saw her." Bart said, anguish making his voice squeak. He averted his eyes, then looked back.

"The coroner says she had an aneurysm. She probably didn't even feel it." Morris' eyes looked at him sympathetically. "I don't know if that makes it better or not, Mr. Jackson." He fingered the envelope and avoided Bart's eyes, obviously giving Bart room to grieve.

Bart looked at him, eyes burning. "Yes and no. At least she didn't suffer." He dropped his gaze to his hands. They looked huge to him, and he felt disconnected to them. They lay in his lap, limp, like rubber gloves. "This must not be a favorite part of your job."

Morris started. "Not really. I'd rather bust a hundred creeps for speeding or dealing drugs than tell friends that other friends have left them." He tapped the envelope. "We found this in Ms. Walker's office. It's addressed to you." He tapped it against his fingers for a moment, eyeing Bart, then handed it to him. "You'll have to sign that you have possession of it, but it's yours, free and clear."

"Alright." Bart took the envelope, and buried his face in it. Fighting to keep the sobs from tearing out his throat, he sighed hugely and croaked, "Where do I sign?"

"The desk sergeant has the papers. Take your time, Mr. Jackson." Morris stood up, and patted Bart's shoulder. His hand dropped back into his lap. "We don't suspect foul play. Ms. Walker died of natural causes. At least you know she went peacefully, not suffering. There are dozens of ways to leave this life, as I'm sure you know. Ninety nine percent are horrible, the kinds of things you wouldn't wish on an enemy, let alone friends."

"Thank you, Sergeant. I'll try to remember that." Bart said, his head dropping. Tears fell on the envelope, blurring the beloved handwriting. *If something happens to me, give this to Bart Jackson.*

Morris walked back to his desk, watching the big black man struggle with his grief in the lobby. He watched Bart get up, drag himself to the desk, and struggle to write his name. Morris thought about offering him a ride home, but if he made it to the station thinking Jenny Walker was dead, he could make it home too. Shaking his head, Morris checked *Deliver envelope to Bart Jackson* off his to do list and went onto the next item.

Bart sat out in his car in the police department parking lot, gripping the steering wheel so hard his knuckles turned white. His mind just couldn't grasp Jenny's death. He thought of the petite strawberry blonde, and saw her laughing at some joke he had told. His heart leaped and fluttered like a bird in a cage.

He hadn't exactly been in love with her, but he would miss her friendship. She was one of the few members he didn't have to explain things to more than once. She always knew how he was feeling, too, and did what she could to cheer him up, if he needed cheering up. He never had to tell her he needed her, she just knew and showed up. Like a personal radar. He would miss that.

He started the engine, and flipped the dome light on. Pulling the envelope out of his pocket, he opened it carefully, knowing that he would keep it forever. Carefully unfolding the letter, he clasped the paper to his breast, as if it were physically her, and hugged it. With a sob, he positioned the letter in the dim light from the overhead lamp, and began to read.

Dear Bart,

If you're reading this letter, it means that I am no longer around to cheer you up. I'm sorry to cause you grief, my friend, but I'm assuming it was time for me to go, and I hope I didn't suffer too much.

Just to focus on business for a minute - this letter appoints you executor of my estate. I have no family to speak of, just a father around somewhere. I don't even know who he is, let alone where he is. My family has been the coven for so long... anyway, you are now in charge of my estate.

The key to my house in town is under the third garbage can on the right next to the garage. It is taped to the bottom, and has an invisibility spell on it. Only you and I can see it. Dispose of the things inside the house as you see fit. The only request I make of you in regards to the house is to let each coven member choose one thing inside to remember me by, but please cleanse them first. I have no wish to be kept on this plane. I must move on, as you know everyone must. Whether you keep the house or sell it is your decision, but I feel that if you sold it, the profits would benefit the coven. It is a nifty little place, even if I do say so myself.

The flower shop is now yours. Yeah, I know you don't care for flowers, but I made a tidy profit from it every month, and the money will come in handy for the coven. Find somebody to run it for you if you don't want to give up the restaurant business - I have an apprentice who would make a good manager. Her name is Maggie Wassanbloom, and she is one of the few natural earth witches I have ever seen. At least offer her the job - if you want to make arrangements with her to purchase the shop on time payments, I would consider the matter well taken care of.

All of these things are suggestions, my friend. I'm sorry to leave you with such a chore, but I trust nobody else with things like this. Please tell everyone I said bye, ok? I'll see them again someday, I'm sure.

Now for a personal note: I'm sorry I never tried to pursue you beyond our handfasting. I've been in love with you for years, but was too chicken to mention it. Pity. I think we would have made a hell of a couple, Bart. Bye now, and remember there's always a someday. If it doesn't come in this life, it'll come in the next.

All my love,

Jenny

Bart sniffed. "Jenny, you crazy mixed up kid. If I'd known you felt that way..."

He started his car, and drove out of the parking lot, clutching the letter to his heart. His mind swam with visions of her.

"Randy," a voice said accompanied by the lightest of taps on his face. "Randy, time to rise and shine."

"Maggie?" He croaked, sitting upright. His brain felt all fuzzy. The older he got the harder it was to spring into action upon awakening. He needed a minute.

"Right in one, dude." A male voice drawled from nearby. It sounded amused.

Randy yawned. Shaking himself, he said, "What time is it?" He rubbed his face, trying to wipe the grog away.

"A little after 11." Maggie's voice sounded amused. "Is Mom upstairs?"

"Yep. Sleeping, I hope." Randy said, stretching. "She had a hard day." His hand knocked a cushion off the couch as he pulled himself back in from the stretch. "Sorry."

"I saw," Maggie said. "I was watching while getting ready for my date." She picked up the cushion and tossed it back on the couch.

Zeke eyed Randy, smirking. He was leaning against the doorjamb, arms crossing his chest.

Randy thought about saying something to him, but the list of things he could say basically came down to one concept. He just couldn't demand that his girlfriend's daughter's boyfriend show him respect. Not with a straight face, anyhow. But still, it bothered him. Randy wondered if the young man even knew what respect was.

"I'm glad you were there, Randy. I know Mom appreciated it too." Maggie was saying, still standing. She fidgeted with the tails of the transparent blouse she wore. *Good thing she has a tank top on under it*, he thought to himself. He liked the way it flattered her figure. Even though she was not of interest to him, she was attractive. Ruefully he realized he had the same respect for her that he would for his own daughter. That made her off limits.

"No problem. I have enormous respect for your mom." Randy got up. Brushing past Zeke, he continued, "I'm going now." He thought again what a good looking couple they made as he made his way to the front door. *Still a little fuzzy*, he realized.

"Bye." Zeke waltzed over and threw himself on the couch, kicking his boots on the coffee table. Used Kleenex littered the top around his feet, a few of them "foofing" off the coffee table unto the floor from the breeze created by Zeke's boots. The TV clicked on.

Randy left the room, followed by Maggie. Maggie glanced back at the living room. "Sorry."

"It's ok." Randy wanted to say dozens of things to her ranging from 'don't do anything I wouldn't do' to 'maybe you should consider a new boyfriend', but instead just clasped Maggie on the upper arm and kissed her forehead. "Tell your mom I said goodnight, and call me if she needs anything."

"I will." Maggie watched him walk out to his truck, and waited until he got in and started the vehicle before she snapped off the porch light and shut the door.

Randy sat looking at the darkened house, and shrugged. Maggie was perfectly capable of turning the light back on when her young man left. He turned the key and backed out of the driveway.

David knocked on the door to Iris' office, a manila folder in his hand. Impatiently waiting a few seconds, he knocked again.

"Oh, for Pete's sake! Come in!" Iris yelled, a note of irritation in her voice.

David smirked, and opened the door. Quickly schooling his expression, his face was a mask of unconcern as he entered Iris' presence. Tapping the folder, he said, "Lilly is not going to work out."

Iris lay on the floor in her office, wrapped in her black robes and sprawled out on an exercise mat. A Yoga video played silently on the TV facing her desk. "Figures." Iris straightened her robes. Yoga always messed them up.

"Does that help you?" David asked, watching her body as it flinched and wiggled into a more comfortable position. "Why don't you wear clothes designed for that? I doubt if Hakon would care."

"Yoga is a relaxing exercise for me. You know that. It keeps my limbs supple." Iris said, her voice exasperated. She arranged her robes so they covered her and fixed him with a "you're in my light" stare. She had one knee bent and the robe that was draped over it slid off, exposing that one leg from toes to hip. Iris didn't notice. "Besides, how would YOU know what Hakon would care about or not? I will exercise in whatever garb i choose, thank you."

"Hmm." David's mouth twitched, his eyes on her legs. He averted his gaze before she truly noticed where his eyes were and said, "Like I was saying, Lilly is not a possibility. She has a teenaged daughter. I am pretty sure that means she is not a virgin."

"And therefore useless to our purpose." Iris crossed the room to her desk and sat down behind it. Drumming her fingers on the desktop, she fixed him with a thoughtful stare. "I've been thinking, Jinx. It may be possible to use her anyhow. She does have demon blood. That has to count for something."

"Not necessarily. Her blood only counts for one criterion. You know the main reason we're looking for a virgin is the disastrous results of the last attempt." David said, laying the folder on her desk. "The log clearly blames the last results on the fact your mother was not a virgin."

"Yeah, yeah. I know." Iris swept the folder into her desk drawer without looking at it. "Is there anything at all we could use?"

David sighed, and leaned on the desk. Crossing his arms, he said, "The daughter is a possibility. I don't know if she's a virgin or not." He eyed her speculatively. "I could find out for you."

"Do that. I've got a few ends here to tie up." Iris pulled a logbook closer. "I have to plan the next ritual. Send Deirdre in on your way out, will you? I have to lay out the format."

"Sure." David shoved off from the desk and made his way to the door. He turned in the doorway, and took one last look at Iris. Her head was bent over the book; she didn't even notice he was leaving. He licked his lips. Maybe she wouldn't notice if Deirdre was a little late.

"And don't make no plans for Deirdre. You can play with her later." Iris said as he stood there. She turned and nailed him with a dark look. "Just because she is the ritual sex object does not mean she is available for all types of cretins like you. Her services are for the coven's benefit, not personal gain." She banged her fist on the desk. "Every time you use her, you cheapen her purpose." She dropped her head back to her paperwork. "I don't suppose you care about that."

"Oh, I care. But she's better than nothing, and easily accessible. It's not like I can have you..." David said, flushing red. He whined, "A growing boy like me needs an outlet."

"Well, find another one, will you?" Iris turned back to her desktop. "Or at least, work on your timing."

David scowled at her back, then went to find Deirdre, softly shutting the door of the office shut behind him. *Just for that*, he thought, *you can wait a few minutes for her.*

Iris stared at the door for a second, then clapped her hands together in a prayer. *Hakon, if you want me to eliminate Jinx, let me know.* She went back to her paperwork. Hakon knew where she was. She just needed to wait.

Honey Cormae poured a cup of water into the cauldron on her table and lit the burner under it. The willowy brunette stared at the water for a moment, wishing it would start steaming already. Raising blue eyes to the ceiling, she sent a thought to Bart. *It's begun.*

Striking a match, she lit the white candle on the altar. "Please bless this ritual with success, O Goddess. Thou knowest how important it is." Lighting the blue candle next to it, she intoned, "Please help me in this quest, O God of protection." Shaking out the match, she bowed her head and prayed for a moment.

Honey opened the bag of sage and sniffed it. The pungent sweet smell drifted up, assailing her nostrils. She grinned at the smell. "Sage! The mainstay for protection." She sprinkled the herb over the water and stirred it with a bark-laden branch. Other ingredients dotted the table here and there, all within arm's reach. She picked up a small vial filled with red liquid.

"Cherry wine, to make the contact agreeable." Honey measured out a tablespoon and added it to the cauldron. The mixture steamed obligingly. She picked up another container, this time a square covered dish. Taking the cover off, she pulled out a small piece of moss.

"Moss, so that the contact will stick to the subject." Adding the moss to the cauldron, she stirred it again. Woodsy steam billowed out and drooped over the lip.

In turn she added orris root, dandelion stems, witch hazel, licorice oil, and 2 hairs from a black female cat, stirring the concoction after each ingredient was added. Picking up a wand, she waved it over the cauldron. She began to chant.

"Sage and wine, lend your aid. Orris root, dandelion, and witch hazel, combine with the licorice to assist my cause. Hairs of the cat, send forth your vessel to protect Lilly Wassanbloom and her daughter Maggie. Ingratiate yourself with the women, vessel, and protect them against evil with the help of this potion."

Taking a ladle, she dipped out some of the potion and poured it into a bowl, straining it through her fingers. Taking the bowl, she laid the spoon on the table, and walked over to a cat carrier. Opening the cage, she placed the bowl in the cage. A black cat darted forward and began to lap the contents. When the cat had finished, Honey shut the door of the cage and carried it to the back door.

Stepping out onto the porch, she set the cage on the deck and opened the door. "Go," she said. "Go and fulfill your duty."

The cat darted out of the cage and ran off to the woods. Honey picked up the carrier and took it back into the house, closing the door and shutting off the porch light behind her. In the total silent darkness that closed in, you'd never know there was a house close by. The woods waited.

Lilly woke the next day, none the worse for her fainting spell the night before. Maggie came into the kitchen just as Lilly was sipping the last of her coffee.

"Morning," Lilly said as Maggie helped herself to a cup. "Do you have to work today?"

"Yeah." Maggie added sugar and cream to her coffee. She sat at the breakfast bar, cup held in both hands. Steam rose from the cup. Maggie smiled just a little, then said, "Mom, do you ever get the feeling that something is not quite right?"

Lilly stared at Maggie for a second, then said, "Yes." She stared for a second longer, then dropped her gaze. She mumbled, "Occasionally." She stared into her coffee cup as intently as a tea leaf reader, except it was coffee. *Coffee grounds lie*, she thought to herself, then lifted her eyes to Maggie's face.

"What are you saying?" Maggie asked, raising the steaming cup to her lips, meeting gaze for gaze.

Lilly looked at her daughter. "Most people like me would call that a premonition." She reached over and shut the coffee pot off.

Maggie giggled. "Are you trying to say I'm developing psychic powers like yours?" Maggie watched her mother avoid her eyes.

Lilly put her coffee cup in the sink. It was still half full. "Just know that I'm here, and I know what it feels like. If you ever want to talk about it..."

"Mom," Maggie said, exasperated. She set the coffee cup on the counter. "Do you realize you've been looking for signs in me for as long as I can remember?" She pulled her robe closer around her body. "Did it ever occur to you I might be just an average ordinary type of person?"

"Many times," Lilly said, placing a comforting hand on her daughter's shoulder. "I've been praying for you to be 'average and ordinary' since the minute you were conceived. Yet there's a part of me that wants a companion, someone that can do the things I do and not feel ashamed of them."

Maggie put a hand on her mother's and patted it. "I'll be fine, Mom. You'll see."

Lilly laughed and withdrew her hand. "Of course you will, dear. I just wanted you to know how much I care, that's all."

Maggie hugged her mother. "I already knew that, but thanks."

Lilly broke from the embrace, and picked up her purse. "Ok. It's that time, drat it. Remember I'm gonna be out late tonight. Randy's picking me up after work."

"Right." Maggie picked up her cup again, listening as her mother left the house. A few seconds later she heard the car start up, and pull out of the gravel drive. Shaking her head, she took her cup with her as she went to get ready herself. Looking out the window, she saw it was raining. A streak of lightning lit up the sky as she watched.

Maggie listened to the storm rage while she got ready for work. A black cat snuck up on the porch and hunched against the doorjamb, staring intensely at the door opening. When Maggie opened the door to leave, the cat darted inside and hid. Maggie didn't even notice. While she was starting her car and backing into the street, the cat leaped up on the couch and began to dry herself of, leaving damp little dark patches where she lay.

"You're kidding, right?" Maggie said. She had arrived at the flower shop to find Bart Jackson waiting for her in the parking lot. He'd followed her to the door and inside the store. As gently as he could, he told her Jenny was dead. They were now sitting at the work bench n the back of the store, surrounded by the tools of the florist trade.

"Oh, honey," Bart said, "I wish I was." He sighed heavily. His big hands toyed with a tiny pair of florist wire cutters. Opening, closing, opening, closing.

Maggie's head dropped. "Oh, man. I knew today was going to be a bad day. I just had that feeling." She looked back up into Bart's warm dark eyes. "How did it happen?"

"The doc says it was an aneurysm. She didn't feel a thing." Bart wiped a hand across his forehead. "I wish I could say the same."

Maggie touched his arm. "I'm sorry. I know she was a friend of yours. She used to talk about you once in a while."

"Thanks. I needed to hear that." Bart said, smiling slightly. "Well, now we have to figure out what to do with the store." He looked around as if the solution was waiting to leap out from the corner of the room.

"Probably the most sensible thing to do is figure out who now owns it and see what they want to do," Maggie said, eyes flicking around the store. Things got fuzzy as her eyes teared up. She blinked to clear them. Her nose prickled, and she knew it wouldn't be long before she bawled like a baby.

"That would be me, I guess. Jenny left a note leaving me in charge of her estate since she had no family." Bart pulled a letter out of his pocket and lay it on the table between them.

"Oh." Maggie said, at a complete loss for words. Her eyes stayed glued to the envelope as if she could read the final words of Jenny Walker through the paper.

"She did make a suggestion in regards to the shop. She thinks you'd make a great manager." Bart said, returning the letter to his pocket. "I know this is sudden, but are you interested in the position?"

Maggie tried to blink away the tears. "I don't know. Everything is happening so fast."

Bart laid an arm over her shoulder. "Don't worry about it, my dear. The flower shop isn't going anywhere. Take a day or two and think about it."

Maggie roused herself enough to say, "Aren't you worried about the shop losing money?"

Bart smiled and squeezed Maggie's shoulders. "No. Jenny knew when she gave it to me that flower shops are low on my interest list. We can talk about that later." Letting her go, he looked around the room and said, "I don't suppose the plants would die if left alone for a day or so."

"No. They'd be fine," Maggie replied absently. Her face went blotchy. *Oh, man, here it comes.*

"Good. Then the only things we have to worry about are you and me and how much we'll miss her." Bart's eyes filled with tears too, and he wrapped Maggie in his arms. The next minute they were both crying and leaning on each other for support.

Nicholas Benson watched the display through the picture window, and shook his head. He would miss Jenny too, but his job was clear. *Keep an eye on Lilly and her daughter.*

He ran his hands through his long brown hair. Normally, he presided over the rituals, keeping peace within the coven membership. One look from his piercing green eyes quelled the fiercest arguments, both in the coven and when he was at work as a bouncer. It was an ability he was proud of, and one that he worked at perfecting.

The street was beginning to stir as he sat there. People went about their daily routine as if he wasn't there stalking one of their daughters. Nick shook his head and closed his eyes. Leaning back into the seat, he concentrated on Lilly, and within a few minutes saw her in his mind.

Lilly frowned at the computer screen. The figures she'd just entered wouldn't add up. She checked the calculator; it was all fine there. Quickly she ran through the figures again. Yep, they were right.

"I just don't get it," she mumbled to herself. "Why won't you add up?" She escaped from the program and started it again. "Maybe this will do it."

Once again she input the data, and came up with the same figure. "Rats." Sighing, she escaped the program again. Clicking on the start menu, she pulled up the 'find' dialog box, and typed in 'cache'. She erased the files, then typed in '*.tmp', and cleared those files too. Then she emptied the recycle bin and rebooted the system.

Picking up her coffee cup, she sipped it while the computer booted up again.

Nicholas opened his eyes, and glanced at the flower shop. Bart and Maggie were still hugging each other. He averted his eyes.

A young man in a leather coat pulled up on a Harley and parked in front of the flower shop. Throwing a leg over, he dismounted and checked his hair in the mirror. Obviously it wasn't as neat as he liked because he whipped out a comb and ran it through. Nick grinned while watching him; it wasn't all that long ago he did the same thing before seeing a girl.

He watched while the young man put his comb away and walked up to the flower shop.

Zeke stopped dead when he saw Maggie through the picture window of the flower shop. Who the hell was that? He watched the big black man rub Maggie's back and his blood boiled. He banged through the door, yelling, "Who the hell are you?"

Maggie broke away from Bart. "Zeke! What are you doing?"

"Defending your honor! Who is this guy?" Zeke said, striding to Maggie's side. He gripped her arm tightly and pulled her behind him. Facing Bart, he growled, "And why was he hugging you?" He glared at Bart.

Bart smiled. Zeke lunged for him. Bart held a hand up, connecting with Zeke's chest and stopping him cold. "Whoa, there, partner. Maggie and me were just talking."

"Zeke!" Maggie said, rubbing her arm. "Would you calm down?" She watched as Bart dropped his hand. Zeke glared at him, jaw clenched, one fist clenched.

"Bart is my new boss, Zeke. Jenny is dead." Maggie said, dropping her head. A tear slid down her nose and dripped onto the floor. "We were just.."

"Talking about her," Bart finished, his voice raspy.

Zeke felt himself flush. "Oh, man. I'm sorry, I thought..." The tension flowed off him like water down a drain, and he felt foolish.

Bart held up a hand, "Don't worry about it. I probably would have thought the same thing." He patted the letter in his suit pocket. "We were just discussing whether we should close down for a day or two until things settle down. I have an appointment with the funeral director in an hour or so, and we can finalize things afterwards."

Maggie looked from Zeke to Bart. "Do you want company?"

"No. That's ok. This is something I have to do alone. For Jenny." Bart said, his eyes wet. "I have a lot of people to notify. She had a lot of friends, but almost no family. I would like to ask a favor of you, though."

"Name it," Maggie said. Zeke looked at her, startled. She sounded so adamant.

"Jenny had no family other than her friends. The pews reserved for the family are going to be almost empty. I would ask you to sit in them for her sake, next to me." Bart said. His eyes flicked to Zeke. "That is, if Zeke here doesn't mind."

"Why would he mind?" Maggie said before Zeke could answer.

"Some people do," Bart said, nodding at Zeke. "Do you?"

"No. Of course not." Zeke said in a shocked tone. "I know how much Maggie cared for Jenny. I would never object to that."

Maggie looked at him, her face soft. Bart shook hands with Zeke, saying, "Thanks, man. Well, I've got to go. Lots of errands to run. Maggie, why don't you just shut down the shop, at least for today. I'll call you later and we'll discuss the other matter."

Maggie nodded. "Alright. I'll be at home. Call me, ok?" She placed her hand on Bart's arm.

"I will." Bart patted her hand, then left.

Zeke watched him walk out to his car while Maggie got her purse. Turning to her, he said, "Are you sure that's all it was?"

"Of course, silly. What else would it be?" Maggie said. She went to the back of the store.

Zeke said, shrugging, "In this day and age you never know."

"What was that?" Maggie yelled from the back room.

"Nothing!" Zeke shouted back, then he went out the back too.

Nicholas followed them to the Movie Hut and watched them rent a movie, then followed them back to the house. Parking a little ways off, he watched the house. All was quiet. The woods buzzed with insects, a comforting homey sound through the open window of his car. He took a deep breath of the earthy aroma, and sighed contentedly.

His cell phone blathered in the silence, scaring him. His heart racing, he picked it up and pushed a button. "Jesus! You scared me!" He held the phone to his ear with one hand while placing the other over his chest as if to stop the racing himself.

"Sorry." Bart replied, his voice gruff. "Were you doing something you shouldn't be doing?"

"Huh? Oh, no. I was just watching the Wassanbloom house. Maggie and Zeke are inside watching a movie. What's up?" Nick said, digging a fingernail into his steering wheel. His left leg began to jiggle, a sure sign of his nervousness if only he'd known it.

"Jenny's public funeral is in two days. The coven will have a private service following the wake." Bart said, his voice tight.

Nick swallowed. "I understand." He had really liked Jenny. The two of them had shared a few late night conversations over the years. He would miss her.

"Make sure you keep an eye on Lilly and Maggie. This would be the perfect opportunity for Iris to make a move," Bart said, his voice getting harder. "I wouldn't put it past them at all."

"Having a premonition?" Nick asked.

"I wish. This is more like a certainty. I just have a bad feeling about this, Nick, and I need your help." Bart's voice shifted a bit from gruff to gravelly, and softened a little through the phone wires.

Nick knew the big black man was fighting back tears. "No problem. I am on the job," he said, soothingly, then hung up and continued to stare at the house. A light came on in the back, bathing the branches overhanging the backyard in the artificial light of the modern world.

CHAPTER THREE

Ordinary eyes seen every day
will now seem to glare your way
even friends and people you know
make the sense of uneasiness grow

Friends become harder to find
events sinister weigh the mind
day by day the symptom grows
until all friends appear to be foes

Hate from others surrounds you now
misunderstandings wrinkle your brow
until comes the day you have to run
at that time, your doom is done

Iris lit the last candle in the set of 7 before her and watched the combined smoke drift out the open window. "Gotcha." Grinning with the feelings of intense satisfaction she felt, she turned at a knock on her door. "Come in."

David threw the door open and walked in, hood back, black robes swaying with his movements. Deirdre Mannis followed him, head bowed, long red hair mussy and hiding her face. Willowy, blue-eyed, and big-breasted, she stood 5'6". The white and green muumuu she wore enveloped her like a cloud, not showing her shape at all. Called "Obedience" within the coven, she was the favorite for rituals and ceremonies. She never complained about the ritualistic bruises that appeared on her creamy white skin nor held back her passions during the ceremonies. Iris admired her performances, and was a touch jealous of the attention her ritual slave received due to her duties within the coven, but everyone had their place.

David grabbed her by the elbow and shoved her abruptly into the room, as if to say *here she is*. The breeze wafted her hair out of her face, and Deirdre glanced at Iris before bowing her head again. Bosom heaving, as if she'd been running to keep up, she awaited her mistress' voice. Her lips were extremely red and slightly swollen, and her complexion was flushed. She looked like she had just rolled out of bed.

Iris looked Deirdre over carefully, then glared at David. "I see you have spent a bit of private time with Obedience, Jinx. Didn't I tell you to play with her later? I need her right now." She placed her hands on her hips and faced him.

David shrugged and released Deirdre, shoving her more towards Iris. "I just couldn't resist her charms." His tone didn't sound the least bit contrite. He faced her defiantly, as if daring her to say something about his infractions.

Iris waved her hand towards the door, turning away from him. "Leave us." She watched him stalk to the door and leave in the windows. She also saw the look of pure contempt he shot towards her just before the door shut. Iris shook her head and mumbled to herself, "Someday I'm going to have to replace him."

"Yes, Acantha." Deirdre said softly, standing at attention. She kept her eyes on the floor, and her head bowed. "You wished to see me?" She clasped her hands in front of her, waiting patiently.

"Yes," Iris said, seating herself behind her desk. "I am planning a ritual and you're going to be a big part of it, Obedience." Gesturing towards a wing-backed, old-fashioned parlor chair on the other side of her desk, Iris invited Deirdre to sit.

Deirdre looked at Iris, her blue eyes shining. "As you wish, mistress." Bowing her head, she walked over and sat in the chair, crossing her legs and placing her hands clasped together in her lap. She sat with her head down, not looking at her mistress.

"The ritual will be in two days time. Make yourself ready. Do not allow any contact with other coven members. You must be pure starting now or the ritual will not be effective. Do you understand?" Iris said, tapping a key on her laptop.

"I understand." Deirdre said, fidgeting a little.

"What's the matter?" Iris glanced at Deirdre The girl looked flustered. She turned back to her screen.

"Permission to speak, mistress." The girl still didn't look up at her, just fidgeted with her fingers in her lap.

"Granted." Iris moved her eyes from the screen and watched her servant. The browbeaten manner of the girl pleased her.

"How do I address those who require my services?" Deirdre said, her eyes down. "I am expected to render services if asked according to my role within the coven."

Iris looked at Deirdre. "That is true but not when preparing for a ritual. Tell them that you are under my instructions to not sully yourself with them until the ritual. If they get sticky, send them to me. I'll set them straight."

"Yes, mistress." Deirdre rose from the chair, bowed and left the room. Iris didn't even wait until Deirdre left before she opened her journal.

> *I have just released the first of three conversion spells upon poor Lilly's head. It shouldn't take long before she begs us to help her.*

I am still convinced that Lilly could be of use to us. If not her, then her daughter. Jinx is supposed to be figuring out if the daughter is a virgin or not. Of course, knowing him, the daughter may not remain a virgin if he finds her. If that becomes the case, I shall take great pleasure in watching Hakon destroy him.

I still wish I could be the vessel. Must see if Hakon will allow it. That way at least we'd know the child would be pure.

'Iris.'

Iris looked up at the ceiling. The voice had come from nowhere, but she knew who it was. "Hakon." She crossed her hands in front of her chest, as if laying out for a funeral viewing, and waited for him to speak.

'It serves no purpose for you to be the vessel. We are too close in relationship, my daughter.' The words reverberated through the room, deep and rich and sounding much larger than life even though the speaker was not physically present in the room.

Iris thought for a minute. "Then Lilly would be useless to us." Disappointment rose in her like a tidal wave but subsided just as quickly; she already knew she was not useful for this particular ritual despite being a virgin, and also knew her sister would be not that much different, even if she didn't have the mark of evil like Iris did nor was she a virgin. But the daughter.....

'Except to lure the daughter, yes.' Hakon's voice was still rich and deep, but also softened a little in the gloomy office. Night was falling, and the woods outside the windows was darkening with dusk.

"But wouldn't that be tainted, too? Lilly's daughter is your grandchild," Iris said. *In for a penny, in for a pound*, she thought. She may as well mention possibilities and disasters so they can be planned for and eliminated before the ritual began. Another botched attempt would not go over well with her lord and master.

'These things are not as straightforward as that, my daughter. The further from the source one is, the farther away the demon blood. The blood relationship is not that close to me, since Lilly was tainted from the beginning. She barely has enough demon blood in her to matter, and the daughter has even less, for our purposes practically none at all. It would be safe for me to propagate with the daughter.' Hakon's voice faded. *'See to it.'*

"I will." Iris said, then, "What should I do with Jinx?"

'Leave him to me.'

An emptiness permeated the room. Iris shivered. Hakon was gone. Shaking herself, she went back to her typing. Perhaps she should recruit Mirage to stalk Lilly. The second step was to scare her, so she'd come running to her understanding sister. Iris sat back with an evil grin on her face. Time was running out.

Lilly dropped her purse and keys on the table in the hall as she streaked to the phone. "Hello?" Holding the phone to an ear, she sluffed off her shoes with the other and wiggled her toes in glee against the carpet as she waited for the person to answer.

"About time you showed up, woman. Even us stalkers have a life, you know." A deep menacing voice snarled. "What took you so long to get home from work?"

"Who is this?" Lilly stammered. Her palms grew clammy, and she wiped one of them on her clothes. Anger warred with terror as hot spikes of adrenaline shot through her chest. She swallowed nervously, looking frantically in all the corners as if the man were going to materialize in front of her.

"Never mind who this is. The point is…I'm watching you." The line went dead.

Lilly hung up the phone, her hands shaking. *Probably just some nut*, she thought to herself. "Just a wrong number," she said out loud. She walked to the window and peeked out into her yard. *Nobody out there but the little birdies*, she thought as she tucked the curtains closed again and went to the couch, sitting down and sinking gratefully in the overstuffed cushions.

A black cat leaped to the couch beside her and meowed. Lilly jumped, a hand flying to her chest. "Jesus! You scared me!" She ran a hand along the cat's back. "Where did you come from, kitty?"

The cat pushed up against Lilly's hand, purring. Lilly scooped the cat up, and headed for the kitchen. "Let's see if we can find something that passes as cat food." The black female lay in Lilly's arm, purring as Lilly opened the refrigerator.

Nicholas watched from the street as Lilly carried the cat into the back of the house. He didn't know if the feline made him feel better or not. What would a cat do if the legions of hell descended on the house? He pulled out a notepad and pencil. Time to take notes. He rummaged around in his knapsack for a clip on book light.

Deirdre walked through the mansion's hallway, on her way to the kitchen. Iris had demanded she spend time preparing food for her family, as a prelude to the ritual. Deirdre's robes swished as she walked, and she smiled.

She loved her job. It wasn't every day you got to hang out naked for a job, and even when you did wear a robe, there was nothing on under it. She reveled in her youthful body, and was glad the coven found a way to use it. She'd peel a mountain of potatoes as long as she was useful in some other way too.

She felt her hair bounce as she walked, and tossed her head. She'd been chosen for this position within the coven, and spent time practicing her role as unwilling victim for the sex rites. In two days, she planned on giving a master performance. She hurried to the kitchen, intent on finishing quickly so she could spend the afternoon practicing.

Jinx watched Deirdre bounce by from the shadows of a doorway. He licked his lips and followed her.

"Maggie?" Lilly called from the kitchen. "Are you home?" A search in the fridge revealed nothing that would pass as cat food, not even lunch meat graced the shelves within. She opened the cupboard that housed the canned goods.

"Yeah!" came from the den. "Zeke and I are watching a movie."

"What about work?" Lilly asked, opening a can of tuna fish for the cat. She freed the lid and compressed the lid within the can to drain the liquid. Taking a paper saucer out of the same cupboard, different shelf, she forked drained tuna onto the plate and placed it on the floor, depositing the cat in front of it. The cat dug in, growling a little in aggressiveness.

Maggie walked into the kitchen. "Hey! Where'd the cat come from?" She looked it over, careful not to disturb it while the kitty tore into the tuna fish. "It's kinda cute." Cocking her head, she said, "It's kinda young too. What would you say, about 6 months old?"

"I thought she was yours," Lilly said. She watched the cat dig in, and looked at her daughter. "Maggie! What's wrong?"

"Oh, mom!" Maggie said, tears running down her face. "Jenny's dead." She leaned on the counter and deflated a little, like she was tired of holding up a good front.

"Jenny? Who's Jenny?" Lilly said, her heart racing. The cat finished and ran off into the rest of the house.

"My boss at the flower shop. Don't you remember? We had her over for dinner a few times," Maggie said, shoving her hands in her pockets. "I can't seem to stop crying. It comes and goes." She glanced up at her mom, and said, "Zeke refuses to leave me until he's sure I am ok."

"Oh, yeah," Lilly said in a bemused voice. "Sorry to hear it." She stared at the cupboard like it was a new thing in the room. After a moment, she turned her gaze to Maggie, then stared back at the cupboard.

Maggie searched her mom's face. "Are you alright?" Maggie's heart lurched. For a split second a complete stranger had looked at her from her mom's eyes, and she felt an uneasy lump in her chest that had nothing to do with Jenny.

Lilly wrenched her eyes back to Maggie's face. "Of course. I feel fine." She grinned. "We need more tuna. I gave the last can to the cat."

"Oh, ok," Maggie said in a low voice. She took a deep breath and said, "To tell you the truth, mom, I was hoping for…"

Lilly stared at Maggie, one eyebrow raised in a 'what do you want now' way. Maggie swallowed and glanced at the den. Canned laughter from the movie Zeke was watching floated through the doorway.

Maggie looked back at Lilly.

"What?" Lilly said, her voice edgy. "People die, right? It's not like it never happens." She tossed her hair and said airily, "I have to go get ready. Randy will be here soon, and suddenly I can't wait to see him." She walked out of the kitchen, humming to herself.

Maggie watched her, puzzled. She didn't move when Zeke came up and put an arm around her. "I heard, baby," he said as she turned her face to his chest and cried.

The small church in town had very few people in it considering how popular Jenny was. People on the street said all the time what a wonderful person she was, and loved her flower shop, but hardly any of them came to her funeral. All told there were about two dozen friends scattered throughout the pews. Maggie, Bart and Zeke sat in the Family pew, them being her family, and listened to the preacher extol Jenny's life to anyone who would listen.

Maggie held Zeke's hand all during Jenny's funeral, grateful that he at least was with her. Increasing worry over Lilly distracted Maggie during the services. Bart's quiet dignity next to her didn't even distract her; she was too worried. She needed to talk to someone, but didn't know whom to turn to.

"Hey. You ok over there?" Bart whispered, startling her. Mutely, she nodded. Bart took a good look at her face, and whispered, "We'll talk later." He patted her hand, and turned his attention back to the preacher. Maggie hung her head.

Zeke glanced at Maggie, and patted her hand too. He was bored, but knew this was his place. Maggie needed him, and that was good enough for him. He tried to overlook the fact that he'd worn his leather jacket. Perfection wasn't his thing. Anybody who thought it was had another think coming.

Lilly searched her face in the hand mirror she pulled out of her purse. "What's wrong with this picture?" she asked the face in the mirror. "You should be at Jenny's funeral, supporting your daughter, and look where you are." She looked around her bedroom. The personal things spread around looked both familiar and alien, as if she was looking at stuff with déjàvu eyes. The stuff was both hers and not hers. She shook her head as if to clear it. Maybe Maggie would forgive her if she appeared at the wake. Hurriedly, she began to dress.

The black cat watched from the middle of the bed. Nonchalantly, she stretched out, taking up as much space as she could. Her green eyes followed Lilly around the room, pausing to glare at the phone when it started to ring.

The church had a meeting hall off the kitchen that was pressed into service for Jenny's wake. Tables and chairs were laid out in rows, each table covered with white paper off a roll and taped to the ends of the table so it wouldn't roll back up. Folding chairs sat around the tables, mostly empty, as people arrived for the food and to reminisce about Jenny. Flower arrangements made beautiful centerpieces. Fitting display for a florist. Stark white walls, linoleum floor; the room was huge. The acoustics were good, and words reverberated off the walls. So far the table settings outweighed the mourners. Folding chairs sat empty all over the room.

The ladies of the church prepared food and set it on the counter for people to serve themselves. Fried chicken, spaghetti salad, chopped salad, egg-plant lasagna, veggie trays, deviled eggs, fruit trays, and a crock pot of chili complete with all the fixings (including dinner rolls) was almost ready to be served. So far nobody had touched it, almost as if nobody wanted to be first. It was a veritable mountain of food for so few mourners.

Maggie wedged herself into a corner at the wake, not feeling like talking to anyone. She picked the one chair farthest away from everyone at the most remote table there was in the room. She was so worried. She sighed and sipped her punch, pretending to be totally absorbed in her fingernails and hoping people would leave her alone.

"Where's Zeke?" a deep voice said, startling her.

Maggie looked up at Bart. "He's outside smoking. I'm afraid he's not much for funerals or wakes."

"At least he came," Bart said, "right?" He held his tie in one hand, and pulled out the chair next to her with the other. Raising his eyebrows, he indicated he was going to sit there.

"Right," Maggie answered, looking down. She didn't mind if he sat next to her.

Bart cleared his throat. "I noticed your mom didn't come. I thought she would, at least for your sake." He sat down and pulled the chair in, tucking his tie in his suit coat pocket. "I mean, even if she didn't really know Jenny, she knows you." He folded his hands in front of him on the table.

"That's what I don't understand. Mom is usually so supportive. I don't know what's wrong with her," Maggie said. "She's been acting strange the last few days."

Bart looked up at the ceiling and closed his eyes. "I don't know, either, but I'll talk to her if you want me to."

"What would you say?" Maggie asked, exasperated. "Thanks for not coming? Thanks for leaving your daughter alone to suffer?" She clasped her hands together and clenched them in her lap. They began to tremble with the force of her grip. Her nose got all prickly, and she knew she was going to cry again. She swallowed painfully and forced it back down again.

Bart looked startled, then said, "I guess not." He sat back and crossed his legs, one hand drumming his fingers on the table. "When did you notice she was different?"

"When I told her Jenny died, she said that people die all the time, or something like that. That's not like her." Maggie's eyes went unfocused for a second, then cleared. "I wonder if Randy has noticed a difference. He went out with her last night."

"Randy James? I think I saw him a few minutes ago." Bart said, scanning the crowd for Randy's face.

"That's another thing. How come he's here, but she isn't?" Maggie said, her voice strained. She clasped her hands tighter, barely noticing when Bart gestured Randy over. Randy nodded in his direction and headed over. He swung by the drink table and carried over a few sodas too. He set the drinks on the table.

"Randy. Good to see you," Bart said, shaking hands with him.

"You too. Hi, Maggie," Randy said, smiling at her. He sat down next to her, his eyes on her hands. "Here. You're gonna cut off your circulation." He reached over and pried her hands apart and laid them one on top of the other in her lap. He put a Mountain Dew in front of her on the table, unopened. "How you holding up, girl?"

"I'm not," Maggie said, and began to cry. "I'm not doing well at all."

Randy placed an arm around her shoulders and let her cry. She buried her face in her hands. Bart shot Randy a significant look and left, intent on finding Zeke before Zeke found them. Nobody needed a scene today.

Zeke was outside, a cigarette drooping from his hand while he stared up the street. His jacket hung open, the collar spiked to stand up. Shaking his head, he took a drag as Bart walked over to him. "Nice funeral," he said by way of greetings.

"I think Jenny would have liked it," Bart answered. "I'm glad you came with Maggie." Bart took the opportunity to size Zeke up on the sly.

"Yeah, well, you know," Zeke said, embarrassed. "She needed somebody. Lilly basically blew her off." He scuffed a foot on the ground. "I just don't get it, man. Lilly used to be the greatest mother, you know? She's gone whacko or something lately."

"You mean this behavior isn't normal?" Bart asked, pretending to be surprised.

"Not in the least. She's acting totally weird, man. Almost like someone switched twins on us." Zeke said, dropping his cigarette and grinding it out with his boot. "I know it depresses Maggie, and I just don't know how to fix it." He looked down the street again. "I keep expecting Lilly to show up, you know? To say...whatever." He glared down the street and said, "I'd probably still be here waiting for that come judgment day if she's the same as she was earlier."

"I see," Bart said. Zeke didn't look like he was wrapped that tight at the moment either. Bart could see the young man was agitated, and wondered if it was all because of Maggie.

"No, I don't think you do. Lilly has gone off the deep edge, dude. She's not even the same person anymore," Zeke said loudly. "She used to like me. Now she looks at me as if I was a fungus on her boot, and I don't like it. She cornered me yesterday and wanted to know if I had 'banged' her daughter yet." He lit another cigarette. "It was weird."

"Sounds like it. Here," Bart handed Zeke a business card. "This has my cell phone number on it. Call me anytime."

Zeke eyed him suspiciously. "Why?" He held the card between his thumb and forefinger like it was contaminated.

"I care," Bart said, pretending offense. "Is that a crime?" He ran a hand down his sleeve as if wiping off deceit. "I have several reasons to be interested, you know. For one thing, I am now Maggie's boss, and I have plans for her. Jenny suggested that I sell Maggie the shop, and I want to make sure Maggie can handle it. Plus I'm worried. Maggie is far more upset over the way her mother is acting than she looks, and I don't like the stress levels I see in her." He shrugged. "Just keep me posted, ok?"

"Ok," Zeke said, pocketing the card. He stared at Bart for a minute, as if measuring his worth. He visibly relaxed, and said, "Thanks. I appreciate your offer. I'm sure she will too."

"Couldn't ask for anything more," Bart said. He clapped Zeke on the shoulder. "Gotta run. I have to talk to everyone at least once for Jenny's sake. Later."

Zeke watched him leave, then turned his eyes back to the street as if searching for someone. *This day just keeps getting stranger and stranger,* he thought as he dropped the cigarette, half smoked, crushed the butt with his foot. With a last longing look up the street, he went back inside the funeral home in search of Maggie.

The time has come, my wayward sister
To grow afraid of those you trust
Suspicions fill your mind and heart
Self-protection becomes a must

As friends and family fall away
All those people you once knew
One thought grows stronger evermore
Only a sister can remain true

Iris finished the chant and started again. Lighting a candle, she wisped the smoke towards the ceiling, her words carrying the spell away. She recited the chant a third time, falling back on her heels and kneeling on the floor in front of the altar, her back to the rest of the room. Swaying to the chant in her mind, she let herself drift until she felt the spell land on Lilly.

"You look so pretty when you're in that position," a soft voice said behind her.

Startled, she opened her eyes, and turned her head. "Damn lucky thing for you the spell was completed, Jinx, or I would have had your head." She gathered her robe in her hands, preparing to get up.

"Whoa! No need to get nasty." Dave held up his hands in a defensive gesture, making no move to help her to her feet.

Iris got up and stalked to her desk, robe flowing behind her as if she was standing facing a breeze. "I want you to leave me alone, understand? It's not proper." She flopped in her office chair, and pulled it under the desk, effectively hiding her shape from his view. Once she got it as she wanted it, she glared at David.

"I don't see anything wrong with telling a woman she's pretty," Dave said, sulking. "Even you." He crossed his arms over his chest, wrinkling his robe. The hem rode up in front, showing his loafers. "Most women like being told they're pretty."

"I am not most women. I am your superior in the coven, and you know propagating is not in my destiny," Iris said, her voice strong. "I have to remain pure, damn it, and you are always going too far." Her fingers traced the edges of her desk blotter as she glared at him.

"What are you going to do, fire me?" Dave asked, mockingly. His eyes watched her fingers move along the edge, and he swallowed.

He stood defiantly in front of her, his eyes boring into her face. She watched a thin line of blue smoke trickle through a crack in the floor and wind up his leg. She smiled. "I won't have to do a thing. My father will protect me," she said.

The smoke tightened around his leg. He looked down, mouth open. He tried to move and found that leg attached to the floor. Futilely, he stopped and just stood there, looking at her with a calculating gaze.

"Now, you have a choice. You can either choose to leave me alone from now on, or take your chances with my father. What will it be?" she asked, leaning on the desk, supporting her weight with her arms.

Dave looked from her to his leg, then back at her. "Ok. I'll leave you alone." The smoke receded back into the floor, and he sighed. He stepped off to the side as if to get a better look at her.

"Now that we've got that taken care of, what news do you bring?" Iris asked. She sat at her desk like nothing had happened, watching his face.

Dave blinked and said, "Maggie is a virgin. I'm certain of it. Plus, the Bright Star coven is short a member. One of them died the other day. Her funeral was today. I heard through the grapevine it was wonderful but sparsely attended."

"Perfect. Do you know what that means?" Iris asked, excited. Her eyes sparkled in the candlelight.

"No opposition," Dave said matter of factly. The air in the room grew colder. David pulled his robe closer.

"Exactly. The second blow has been struck. Lilly should start fearing everyone within a few minutes. She will soon feel that I am the only one she can trust." Iris chuckled. The sound carried through the room, bouncing off the walls and growing deeper in pitch, as though there was more than one person laughing.

Dave looked around, his heart racing. "Did you hear that?" He felt a chill run up his spine and shivered.

Iris looked up, her eyes glazed. "Yes. My father loves it when a plan comes together."

Dave cringed. "I see. Ok. Well. I guess I'd better be going." He began to edge towards the door.

Iris closed her eyes and began to sway, humming under her breath. She was so involved in her own little ritual, she never even noticed when Dave left the room and shut the door softly behind him.

Deirdre shook her head. Things looked fuzzy. She laid the paring knife on the counter, rubbed her eyes and blinked. A dark robed figure beckoned to her from the kitchen doorway. Her heart lurched but she ignored it.

"Obedience. Come." She mutely followed. She did not ask where he was taking her; that was not her place. As always, when she was addressed by her coven name, she was forbidden to speak or resist. So she went where he led, silent.

The two walked silently down the hallway, the girl following the shadowy figure through the gloom. They stopped at the door of the altar room, and he opened the door. Gesturing her inside, he slipped the door closed and locked it. Taking her elbow, he escorted her to the altar and helped her lay on it. His hands lovingly removed the symbol of chastity Iris required her to wear. He placed it beside her on the altar.

Deirdre lay back, allowing him to arrange her in the position he required. She was familiar with all the men in the coven, but this one cowed her. She didn't know what to make of him, and was not entirely comfortable with him, but couldn't ask him anything due to her position. She wondered if it was time for the ritual yet, and felt a twinge of regret that she'd not had time to practice. She'd just have to do the best she could. Her breath hitched as she prepared her mind.

He held her ankles together, tying them loosely with a black silken cord. He then moved to her side, one after the other, stretching her arms straight out from her sides on the granite surface, but not tying them down. He laid a hand on her forehead, murmuring some words she could not quite hear. She felt drowsy and closed her eyes. Immediately, she fell into a deep sleep.

The shadowy figure studied the sleeping girl for a moment, then swiped back the hood that hid his face. Hakon's blue complexion glowed in the candle light, his yellow eyes riveted to her face. "Now we begin," Hakon said, his voice soft. He waved a hand over her body. A blue smoky film emerged from his palm, settling over her and concentrating at her side. A flash of red, and the smoke turned into a King Cobra.

The snake nodded at Hakon and settled down, eyes on Deirdre's face. His tongue flicked out every once in a while, but otherwise the snake lay still against her sleeping figure.

"My brother," Hakon said reverently. "Strike when she moves." He placed his hand on Deirdre's forehead again, saying, "I would have much preferred to end your life some other way, my daughter, but this is the avenue I must take. You will be rewarded." He waved his hand and disappeared.

The snake curled up quietly, his head and upper body lying across and on Deirdre's chest. Occasionally, his tongue flicked out while he waited, but those slitted yellow eyes never left her face.

CHAPTER FOUR

"What do you mean she's dead?" Iris asked harshly. "She's not just missing and you are assuming she's dead?" Her office smelled of ginger and cayenne pepper, as if she had been cooking. She had, but it was a summoning spell, not a souffle. Iris was murder in the kitchen; she was a terrible cook.

"No. She's dead. Right there in the altar room," Dave said, his voice strained. He looked terrified, as well he should. If he was blamed for her death, he knew the consequences would not only be immediate, but painful as well. They would hurt. A lot. He swallowed nervously.

"What did she die of?" Iris said, glaring at him suspiciously. She held a BBQ lighter in her hand, preparing to light a black candle on the desk.

"Looks like a snake bite, mistress," Desiree said, her voice submissive. She was a curvaceous 5' 5" with a light complexion, brown eyes, and short curly black hair. She was staring at the floor, as if afraid to say too much.

Iris looked at the young African-American. Iris knew she was 26, and a licensed beautician. Desiree was one of the most sought after beauticians in the area. "I suppose you saw her too?" she spit out, like the brunette's opinion meant nothing.

"Yes, mistress." Desiree said, her hands gripping her robes and her eyes still on the floor.

"I see." Iris sat heavily behind her desk. "So. That means both covens are short a member. Damn." She sat thinking for a moment, then settled her eyes on Desiree. "It is time to take you up on your offer, Chocolate. From this moment on, you are the ritual assistant. Make your preparations."

Desiree stood still for a moment. "Will I be allowed to keep my job?" She fought to keep her voice neutral. Her business was her passion; she had spent the last few years building a reliable clientele, and didn't want to give it up for the Coven.

"Not unless it coincides with your new duties," Iris said, tenting her fingers in front of her. "I have only a very basic knowledge of your occupation. Do you think it would give you the freedom to be available when you're needed?"

"No." Desiree murmured. She flicked her robes a little but otherwise stood quietly.

"Then you'll have to give it up. From now on, the coven and its needs come first." Iris waved a hand at her. "Dismissed." Iris had no qualms about forcing people to rearrange their lives for the Coven. Devotion went without saying, and each member vowed at initiation to serve the Coven in whatever capacity they were called for. Hakon would not accept otherwise, and neither would she.

"But that's not fair! It took me years to get my license. I don't want to give it up." Desiree said, reasonably, a slight edge to her voice. Her nose felt prickly. *This is one of those life-changing decisions,* she thought. *Just like the ones you read about.* Random thoughts about her business building efforts shot through her head, and she shook her head to dismiss them. It didn't matter about the sacrifices she'd had to make. All that effort, wasted. *No use crying over spilt milk,* she said sternly to herself. Belatedly, she thrust her attention back to her mistress.

David grinned behind her. Iris shot him a dirty look, raising her eyebrows at him. He shrugged and looked away. Iris narrowed her eyes at Desiree.

"Your reluctance to give up your occupation is the first step towards your surrender to us. You know the role of ritual assistant. You must be available to all members at all times; it goes with the position. You especially must put on a good show for the rituals." Iris slapped the top of her desk. "You asked for this position if I ever had the need of you. We have an important ritual coming up in a few days, you must be ready. Therefore, your first duty is not just to the coven members. You must humble yourself, my dear."

"How?" Desiree asked, her voice small. She kept her eyes on the floor, but her fists were clenched. She quickly ducked them inside her robes. She felt the anger rise within her, and forced it down. It was true she had volunteered for this position if ever the Coven had need of it, but she had not expected it to be all-consuming. She'd envisioned it more like a role-playing kind of thing (maybe like an acting part) instead of an full-blown occupation. The weight of her position landed like an albatross on her shoulders, and she hunched them as if to support the new responsibility.

"First, quit your job. Then change your robes to those of your station. You are expected in the kitchen within the hour." Iris opened a drawer of her desk and removed a necklace. The shiny gold ankh suspended upside down caught the candlelight. "Wear this too. It symbolizes your unavailability." She gave it to Desiree, and nailed David with a glance. "All who see this will know your favors are not available for now," Iris said. "They will also know your new position." She waved a hand at the girl. "You may go."

Desiree slunk from the room, carrying the ankh in her hand. David watched her go, his eyes watching her body under the robe. He turned back to Iris as the door shut behind Desiree.

"I don't understand why she's off limits." David said, sitting on the edge of the desk. One leg braced his weight against the desk, the other hooked up and dangled off the edge. He crossed his arms over his chest.

Iris stared at him. "I don't understand why you feel it so necessary to abuse the ritual assistants. Is sex all you think about?" She tapped a few keys on her laptop and looked into his face as if surprised he was still there.

David's eyes shifted to her. "Actually, no, it isn't. I spend most of my time thinking about you, but I know you're not interested in hearing about it." His gaze drifted over the books lining the walls, then came back to her face.

"That serves no purpose, Jinx. What you truly want is the one thing I can't give you. Get used to it." Iris said viciously. She pulled her laptop closer, and began to type in ernest. "It would be most useful of you to plan what to do with Lilly when she arrives. It should be sometime tomorrow."

"That soon? What is the plan for her, anyway? She's useless for the ritual." David said, his tone exasperated. "I don't know why you want her in the first place if she's no use to us." He scowled at the floor.

Iris glared at him. "Stop second guessing me. Just believe when I say that she serves a purpose. Now go and think of something to do with her. I'm busy." She ignored him and turned her attention back to the laptop.

David gathered himself and stalked from the room. Just before pulling the door closed behind him, he heard, "Jinx. Do something with Obedience. I don't want the rest of the coven unsettled."

"Yes, mistress," he said, then shut the door. "Don't worry your pretty little head, mistress. I'll take care of Obedience. I'll even plan something special for Lilly, too." With an evil grin, David set off to make preparations, whistling.

Lilly shook her head as if to clear it. She didn't know what was wrong, but she felt fuzzy. Things just weren't *clear* anymore. Wistfully she thought back to just a couple weeks ago; she was so focused then. It seemed like she'd known where she was going and why. Now the details of things were cloudy.

She should have gone to the funeral yesterday. She knew Maggie had needed her support, but in the end hadn't gone. Guilt rose up and peaked, and she flushed in shame. What had she done? Couldn't remember. Suddenly her mind went blank. She stood still for a minute as if waiting for instructions, then pulled out the chair and sat at her vanity. Randy would be there any moment. Lilly couldn't wait to see him.

Maggie paused in the bedroom doorway. "Mom?" She poked her head around the doorway. Seeing her mom inside, she stepped fully into the doorway and waited for her mom to respond.

"What?" Lilly said. Picking up a brush, she began absentmindedly to brush her long hair, like she didn't have a care in the world, nor had guilty, horrible thoughts about herself a few moments ago. She could see Maggie in the mirror, but didn't register the look on her daughter's face.

Maggie said uneasily, "Do you have a minute?" She leaned against the doorjamb, crossing her arms over her chest.

Lilly turned around, facing Maggie. "Sure. What do you want?" She lay the brush on the top of the vanity, and flipped her hair back. Picking up a lipstick, she pulled the top off and twisted the bottom so the burgundy colored tube poked up above the holder. *What a lovely red,* she thought.

Maggie went into the room and sat on the bed. She said, "Are you ok?" She smoothed the covers down with her hands, feeling the smoothness of the bedspread against her palms. She loved the pastel green shade, it always made her feel close to her mother. She noticed that the candle on the bedside stand, usually lit, was not, but didn't think much about it.

"I'm fine. Why do you ask?" Lilly met her daughter's eyes in the mirror, for a split second, then flicked back to her own reflection as she spread the lipstick on her lips. She blotted her lips with a tissue she pulled out of an aqua colored tissue cover and tossed it on the desk.

Maggie watched her mom's eyes flicker between recognition and menace. Her glance flicked to the tissue on the vanity top, and wondered why Lilly just didn't toss it into the trash can next to the vanity. "It's just that, well," Maggie stopped, licking her lips. Suddenly they'd become dry. She rushed on, "I really needed you with me yesterday. How come you didn't come to the funeral?"

Lilly's eyes went blank. "I don't know," she mumbled. Shaking her head, she said more forcefully, "I guess I just didn't want people looking at me." She picked up a mascara tube from the vanity top.

Maggie cocked her head, looking puzzled, then dropped her eyes. "I see." *A lie,* she thought. *I just lied to my mother.* A uneasy feeling settled in her chest. *Something's wrong.*

Lilly lay a hand on her daughter's leg. "It wasn't you, sweetie. To tell you the truth, I intended to go, I really did. I just couldn't seem to get out of the house." A wistful expression came over her face, and she mumbled, "I used to be able to go out in public."

Maggie watched the expression on her mom's face go vague, and felt a stab of fright. "What do you mean?"

"Huh?" Lilly shook her head. "What did you say?" Her hand went back to the vanity and picked up the mascara again, almost as if the hand didn't belong to Lilly at all.

"You said you used to be able to go out in public. What changed?" Maggie searched her mother's face. Lilly's expression changed to a myriad of emotions, then grew cold; like the face of a stranger. "Mom?"

"Nothing changed. Everything is hunky dory." Lilly threw the mascara on the table and picked up her brush. Viciously, she began to yank it through her hair. Suddenly she stopped and stared at Maggie. "Are you going out with what's his name tonight?"

"Zeke?" Maggie said, surprised.

"Yeah, him. Are you going out with him tonight?"

Maggie watched the expressions on her mother's face. Something between envy and anger. Finally, she said, "We were going to go to the movies. Why?"

"I don't trust him. How do I know he doesn't have designs on you?" Lilly turned back to her mirror. She stared at her reflection like she'd never seen it before. "Men always think of one thing. Sex." She turned back and glared at Maggie. "They only want sex! Do you understand that?"

Maggie sat speechless for a moment, then in a small voice, she said, "I thought you liked Zeke."

"I would like him a lot better if he didn't look like a rapper in a rock video. Why does he have to look so scuzzy all the time? Huh? You'd think he'd take some pride in himself." Lilly spat out, using the brush so violently that she pulled some of her hair out. She sat staring at the long strands wrapped around the brush for a moment, then said, "I'm sorry. Maggie. I don't know what's come over me." Listening for a second, she turned. "Maggie?"

The room was empty. Maggie had left. Lilly turned back to the mirror, tears shining in her eyes. "Now look what you've done, you idiot. She'll probably never talk to you again." She buried her face in her hands, and leaned her elbows on the vanity. "What the hell is wrong with me?"

The cat on the bedspread yawned.

Maggie ran from her mother's room, tears streaking her cheeks. Blindly, she grabbed her purse. Snatching the keys off the board in the kitchen, she ran to her car and got in. Not thinking, she started the car and peeled down the driveway. Reaching the street, she turned right and drove, not really knowing where she was going.

Finally she stopped, pulled off to the side of the road, and let the tears come. She had her face buried in her hands, tears falling freely, when a knock at the window scared her. She jumped and dropped her hands. Randy wiggled his fingers at the window and made a rotating sign. She rolled down the window and wiped her eyes with her fingers.

"Hey. What's going on?" Randy said cheerfully. He got a good look at her face, and said, "What's wrong?" He leaned down and propped himself up on the door with his elbows, creating a small space of intimacy.

"It's mom. I think she's lost it." Maggie said, her voice breaking. She looked down. She could feel herself blush. She picked at an imaginary fleck of dust on her jeans.

"Really? Gee, that sounds strange. I mean," he hunkered down next to the car door, "that doesn't sound like her."

"I know. It doesn't. I don't get it." Maggie said, gripping the steering wheel with both hands. "She's like another person, Randy. Have you noticed anything strange about her?"

"Well, yeah, but I thought it was one of those things. You know." Randy said, blushing.

"Like what?"

"Um, well, last night at the restaurant, she accused the waiter of staring at her. She looked him dead in the eye and said, 'Haven't you ever seen anyone order a burger before?' I mean, the guy was really nice, and she treated him like dirt. She kept glaring at him all night." Randy leaned on the window casing. "I thought that was pretty strange. She gets hostile for little to no reason nowadays." He looked towards the direction her car was pointed in, then back at her. "I was going to ask you if you had noticed the same things about her."

"I just caught her staring in the mirror at her own reflection like she didn't know who it was. Do you think she's sick?" Maggie said, easing off the steering wheel. She sniffed; her nose was all stuffed up. She pulled her purse closer and rummaged inside for a kleenex.

"I don't know. We'll just have to keep an eye on her." Randy said, standing back up. "You off to meet Zeke?"

"Yeah. We're going to the drive-in. That's another thing." Maggie said, puzzled. Laying her purse on the seat beside her, she reached forward to turn the key then hesitated, lost in thought.

"What?"

"All of a sudden, she doesn't like Zeke. She says all he's interested in is sex." Maggie started the car and shifted into drive, keeping her foot on the brake. "She used to like him."

"You're right. She's always going on about what a nice kid he is. Hmmm." Randy said, staring off into the distance. "Well, have a good time, Maggie. Don't worry about your mom. I'll stay with her until you get home, ok?"

"Thanks, Randy. Have a good night." Maggie took her foot off the brake.

Randy watched her drive away. Maybe it was time to call Bart again. This kind of drastic change in behavior worried him. Bart should know about this. Randy pulled his phone out.

"I'm telling you, Bart, she's changing as we speak." Randy said into his cell phone a few minutes later.

"Changing how?" Bart asked. His eyes roved the desk, searching for a pen.

"I don't know. She's hostile to Maggie, hates Maggie's boyfriend, and has accused people of 'staring' at her when we go out. She's not the same woman I started dating a few months ago," Randy said, then lowered his voice, "Do you think Iris has anything to do with this?"

"Probably. Obviously the protection spell Honey weaved is not strong enough. I'll ask her to cast a new improved version." Bart finally found a pen in his desk drawer. "I'll get that started right away. In the meantime, keep an eye on Lilly, and keep me posted."

"Will do," Randy said, hanging up.

Bart waited a few seconds, then picked up the phone and dialed Honey's number. "Honey? I need another favor." Briefly, he outlined the plan. "Remember to triple the ingredients and place the talisman somewhere where it can directly influence her. Randy will have her out of the house tonight. Plant it somewhere in the bedroom." He listened then said, "Yes. As soon as possible."

Randy knocked on the door. Almost immediately it flew open, and Lilly came out, slinging her purse over her shoulder. She wore a short skirt and tight blouse, and had her hair tied up on top of her head. Her makeup was spread heavily. Maggie could have picked the outfit for her. Randy raked his eyes up and down and gestured towards the car as if waving the Queen forward.

"Well, come on. We're gonna be late. Where were you?" Lilly said by way of a greeting. She started walking towards the car, her eyes straight ahead.

"I had a flat tire. Sorry." Randy said, following her to the car. "I should have called, but I didn't think it was gonna take that long." He opened the door for her, and once she was settled, he scooted around and got in behind the wheel.

"I guess that can't be helped. So I suppose I should forgive you, right?" She sighed heavily, as if the weight of the world was on her shoulders. She sat with her head bowed, her hands clasped in her lap.

Randy was sure there was something influencing her, and was determined to find out what it was. They drove to the restaurant in almost total silence. Lilly only answered yes or no to anything he said. Randy pulled in the parking lot and parked. Shutting off the car, he said, "Did I do something to bother you?"

"No. Why would you ask that?" Lilly turned to face him, surprise written all over her face.

"You're hardly talking to me. I just wondered if I did something to make you mad." Randy said, patting her hand.

"Oh. No, it's not you. I just must be hungrier than I thought. I can get real crabby sometimes." She patted his hand with her other one and smiled at him. "I'm sorry. I just haven't felt myself lately. Maybe I should shave my head." Reaching into the back seat, she pulled out some contracts from his briefcase and fanned herself with them. "It's sure hot tonight."

A slight breeze wafted towards him, carrying a soft gentle floral scent. He sighed, and got out of the car. He opened the door for her, and extended his hand to help her out. "You know, I'd be happy to help if you need anything." Once she placed her hand in his, he guided her to his side. Tucking her hand in the crook of his elbow, he began the walk towards the door. Leisurely, so they could talk.

She pulled her hand out of his. "When the opportunity arises, I'll be sure to let you know." Airily, she walked ahead of him into the restaurant. Randy ran to catch up to her, fear settling around his heart.

"What do you mean you don't have a reservation? I made the arrangements two damn weeks ago. Now check the list again." Lilly said, staring defiantly at the manager. The contracts she brought from the car fanned furiously towards her face. The force from the breeze generated fluffed her hair out.

Randy felt sorry for the man at the podium. He hovered between despair at her attitude and embarrassment. She was making a scene, and looked like she was burning up. Randy wondered if she was ill; maybe Maggie wasn't that far off the mark. He watched as a flush, like a heat rash, crept up from her bosom and spread over her face.

The manager flushed angrily, and obediently flipped through the pages on his clipboard again. "I'm sorry, ma'am, but there's no reservation for you tonight. I can't even squeeze you in, we're booked solid." He glanced at the couple behind her. "Perhaps if you could take a seat over there, I'll see what I can do. You would be on the Waiting List."

Lilly snapped, "Don't bother. We'll just go somewhere else." She stalked towards the door, calling over her shoulder for Randy while she banged the door open so hard the glass in it shattered, bouncing off the wall and fanning out over the sidewalk in front.

Randy whipped a business card out of his pocket and handed it to the manager. "Have the door fixed and call me. I'll take care of it." He headed for the door, stopping as the manager said something. "What was that?"

"I said," the manager repeated, "What the hell is wrong with her?"

"I wish I knew," Randy replied as Lilly screamed his name from the parking lot. "This is not normal for her." He looked out the front window of the restaurant. Lilly was leaning up against the passenger door, arms crossed over her chest, talking vehemently towards no one. She was so enraged her body jounced while she spoke with the force of her words.

"Well, don't worry about the window, Mr. James. Use the money to get your girlfriend back in whack. She's off her nut." The manager stuffed Randy's card in his pocket, and went on with seating his guests. Randy stared at him for a second before Lilly called him again. Hurriedly, he left.

Honey lay the ingredients she needed on the table, then picked up a cake of pink wax. She placed it in a pan, and set the pan on the stove over another slightly bigger pan. She lit a fire under it, watching as the wax softened, stirring it occasionally. She chanted as she stirred.

Pink wax of this I plea
Mixed with herbs I place in thee
Protect and serve the one in need
Angels above hear my plea

She chanted until the wax was melted, then turned the flame low so it would stay warm but not burn or harden. She started another pan going with a white cake of wax, chanting as it melted.

White wax I ask of you to protect
A woman and daughter, the object
Accept these tokens and project
Your light of truth, please protect

When the wax had melted, she turned the flame down like the first one. She added crushed dragon's blood reed and crushed caraway seeds to the white wax, stirring it well. She crushed garlic and African ginger root together and added it to the pink wax, stirring it well. She then took the white wax mixture and poured it into a glass mold over a wick, chanting:

> *Dragon's blood reed and caraway seeds*
> *Added to white to refute the worst*
> *When burned let the smoke from flame*
> *Return to the sender and break the curse*

She chanted this until the white wax had semi-set. Then she took the pink wax mixture, and poured it over another wick into a different glass mold, chanting:

> *African ginger root and crushed garlic*
> *Added to pink will overcome evil*
> *When burned let the smoke from flame*
> *Return to the sender and banish the evil*

She chanted this until the pink wax had semi-set. She placed both molds in the freezer and cleaned off the table. She brought out some light blue beeswax and spread it out. Using a rolling pin, she rolled the wax flat, then reverently lay some five-fingered grass on it. She rolled it again, setting the five- fingered leaf into the wax while chanting:

> *Five-fingered grass, lend a hand*
> *To the woman of intent and thought*
> *Blend with the light blue of the wax*
> *Bring spiritual awareness and peace*
> *Allow her to see who has wrought the evil*
> *Now plaguing her and her child*
> *Lend her the strength she needs to fight*
> *And the knowledge she needs to protect them both*

On top of the five-fingered grass she lay another layer of light blue beeswax, rolling it until the two layers were blended. She then trimmed the blue wax so the edges were even and lay it aside. She pulled the two candles out of the freezer. Using a hairdryer, she warmed up the molds enough to slide the candles out.

Placing the two candles end to end, wicks opposite ends, she wrapped them in the blue beeswax, cutting off the excess along the seam and on both ends. Working with the wax, she rolled them together until the blue had melded with the pink and white seamlessly. Using a long razor blade, she separated them on the bottoms. She now had two candles wrapped in blue, one white and one pink. She quickly wrapped them in white tulle, tying both with white ribbons. Attaching a card on each one inscribed with the words, "From a Friend - Enjoy!", she placed them in a basket.

Grabbing her purse, she left the house, hoping to get them to Lilly's and in the house before Randy returned.

Maggie yawned while coming through the kitchen doorway. Helping herself to a cup of coffee, she climbed on a stool at the counter. "Morning, mom." The look on her Lilly's face startled Maggie wide awake. "Mom! What is it?"

"Where were you last night?" Lilly snarled. "I was waiting for you, and you never came home. I was worried sick!" She picked up her coffee cup, gulped the steaming liquid, and slammed the cup back on the counter. Hot coffee sloshed over the side of the cup, splashing Lilly's hand. Angrily, she wiped her hand off with a dishcloth and whipped it into the sink. It landed with a squashy 'thud'.

"Didn't that hurt your mouth?" Maggie asked. "It would have burned mine."

"Don't evade the issue. Where were you?" Lilly banged a fork on the counter and glared at her daughter.

"I was at the movies with Zeke. I told you I was going out," Maggie said, defensively. "We always go out Saturday nights."

"I don't give a damn! I don't want you hanging around with that boy anymore!" Lilly stated, her face flushed. She picked up the fork and viciously stabbed a breakfast steak. Tossing it on a plate, she slapped the plate on the counter and glared at her daughter again.

Maggie looked at the steak as if it would bite. "What brought this on? I can remember a few weeks ago how much you liked Zeke." Slowly she lowered her cup back to the counter, suddenly unsure of her mom and how far she would go with her displeasure.

Maggie had never had to worry about those infamous "bad things" kids got beat for in other households where abuse lived. She'd never had to worry bout that before, and the new feelings scared her. She was afraid of her mother, for the first time, and it didn't sit well with her. Not at all.

"Well, I don't like him now. I think he's only interested in one thing, Maggie." Lilly said, her voice rising in tone. "Look at the way he dresses! He looks like a steam punk."

"Mom," Maggie said in a reasonable tone. "We've gone over this before. You know Zeke dresses that way because it's just who he is."

"Like I said, I don't care. Just get rid of him," Lilly said, breaking eggs into a bowl. Beating the eggs viciously with a fork, she dumped them into a pan and pitched the bowl into the sink. Splintered glass flew everywhere.

"Mom! What are you doing?" Maggie ducked as a shard flew at her face.

"Cooking your breakfast! What's it look like?" Lilly slammed the pan on the burner. An empty 'twang' echoed through the kitchen. Blended raw egg sloshed up and splashed over the edge of the pan onto the stove top. Lilly ignored it. She pushed the knob in and held it until the spark caught then placed the fry pan in the flames.

Maggie sighed. "I don't want to get rid of Zeke. I really like him."

"I'm sure. He's probably great in bed too." Lilly stared at the pan as the eggs began to bubble. She ripped holes in the bubbles, scratching the fry pan with the fork.

"I wouldn't know. We haven't gotten that far in our relationship yet," Maggie said softly. Lilly always mentioned not cooking in her pans with metal utensils. She was forever examining them for scratches. *Well, that one had them now,* Maggie thought.

"If you do partake in that exquisite pleasure, use something. I don't want any screaming brat in the house. That stupid cat is bad enough," Lilly said, removing the pan from the flame. She slid an almost cooked omelet on Maggie's plate and stuck a fork in it. "Eat up. You'll be late." She returned to the stove and stared at the flame as if mesmerized.

Maggie glanced at the omelet, fork sticking up like a tower, and swallowed. "I don't think I'm hungry." She could see a glob of uncooked egg right smack in the middle of it, and her stomach turned.

Lilly glanced at her then centered her attention on the flame again. "Suit yourself."

Maggie got off the stool. Stopping at the kitchen entrance, she said, "Are you alright? You're not acting like yourself today." Her heart ached with the accusations about her and Zeke.

Lilly growled, "I'm fine. Go to work or something." She didn't even glance towards Maggie.

Maggie backed away. "Ok. Be careful." She felt like she should say something else, but wasn't sure what. That, too, was new to her. She'd never been tongue-tied with her mom before.

Lilly spun around and faced her. "Oh, yeah. Keep your candles out of my room. I don't know what you've done to them, but they smell. I had to sleep with my window open last night because of the stench." She turned back to the flame. "I put them in the trash, so don't bother looking for them."

"Sorry, mom. I'll keep them away from now on." Maggie left, shaking her head. "I dress the same way Zeke does, mom," she mumbled under her breath. "Does that mean you don't like me anymore either?"

Lilly stared at the flame, unhearing. She watched it rise and fall, sway from side to side, totally fascinated with the life it showed. Finally, she put her hand out as if to caress it.

Iris sat back on her heels. "Father?" she called. The coven was quiet this night. All were preparing for the coming ritual in their own ways. She had ordered the Altar Room scrubbed and the neophytes were working away. Policy said they stayed at their task until completed no matter what, and she had decided that a late evening scrub was just the thing to get them ready for the coming celebrations.

Yes? Hakon's voice resounded in her head. She glanced up at the ceiling as if expecting him to materialize over her head, his voice sounded that close to her. He could have been standing behind her, he was coming through that clear. Hastily, she glanced over her shoulder. Nothing.

"Lilly's getting closer. I can feel her sanity slipping." Iris got up and walked to her desk. Picking up a long-handled lighter, she flicked it to make sure it worked well.

Good. I, too, feel her coming closer to us. Now for the final step.

"Right." She lit a red altar candle, and guided the smoke towards the ceiling. Closing her eyes, she caused herself to go still. Suddenly she began to speak:

> *Hear this, my sister, and heed my call*
> *Run to your destiny, not to fall*
> *Your heart will guide you true to me*
> *Do not rest until my face you see*

Iris concentrated on the words until she felt them reach the target. Leaving the candle burning, she went to her desk. She buzzed the intercom, and spoke into it. "Jinx. Get ready for our guest." Sitting, she watched the candle flame flicker, her fingers tented and a satisfied smile on her face. Echoing behind her, she felt and heard Hakon laughing delightedly.

Maggie returned home from work exhausted. She dropped her keys on the table inside the door at the same time she dumped her purse on the nearest chair. The cat rushed in the room, meowing and rubbing her leg. Maggie scooped the cat up and cuddled it.

"Yeah, you don't know what's happening either, do you?" she crooned to it, rubbing its ears. The cat butted its head against her hand. "I swear, kitty, I don't know what's wrong with mom. She's acting weird. Have you noticed too?" The cat purred.

Maggie deposited the cat into a chair when the phone rang. Snatching it up, she said, "Yes?"

"Hey. What's going on?'" Zeke asked.

Maggie could hear something crinkling in the background. "Nothing much, except Mom is acting stranger by the second. What are you eating?" She glanced up the stairs towards the bedrooms as if she could see her mom's room through the floor.

"Potato chips. Got hungry," Zeke said, his voice a little muffled. "What's Lilly doing now?"

"This morning she pretty much accused me of sleeping with you, for starters," Maggie answered, walking into the den. She sat on the couch and kicked her shoes off. leaning back against the cushions, she brought her feet up and set her toes against the coffee table, knees tented toward the ceiling.

"Really? How interesting," Zeke said, his voice clear again and sounding like he wasn't interested at all. "There's a Gothic festival on channel 67. Are you up for it?"

"I suppose." Maggie covered her eyes with her free hand. "Don't you have anything to say besides that?"

"About Lilly, you mean?" Zeke said, sounding amused. "She's been accusing us of that for about a week now. Nothing new there."

Maggie sat up and leaned forward, propping her elbows on her knees. "Zeke, this isn't the same old thing. I don't know, but somehow the feelings and accusations are getting more desperate. More intense. You know what I mean?" Maggie thumped her fist on her thigh in frustration. "I wish I could explain it better."

"Not really." He sounded resigned. "What's she doing now?"

"Got me. She's not here, but her car is. Maybe she's out with Randy," Maggie said. "He says she's not acting right either." She added as if to say that it wasn't just her that noticed the difference in her mother.

"And how do you know that? A little birdie tell you?" Zeke spat, his voice hard. "I didn't know you were so close to him."

"No, smartass, he did when I saw him yesterday," Maggie shot back. "Don't tell me you're jealous of my mother's boyfriend."

"The stupidity of that remark does not deserve a reply," Zeke said condescendingly. "I'll be over in a few." He hung up.

Maggie stared at the dead receiver, then hung up her end. Shaking her head, she lay back in the silence of the house, listened to nothing, and wondered about her mother.

Zeke drove over to the house, fuming. *Who did that joker think he was?* Zeke could see Randy in his mind's eye. His hands flexed, his biceps bulged against his jacket sleeves, and his jaw set under steely eyes. What he wouldn't give to smash Randy right in the beak! Vividly, Zeke saw himself lambaste Randy, then stand quivering over his prone body, snarling, "Keep your hands off my girl, you son of a bitch!"

Zeke shook his head, and forced himself to let go of the feelings jump starting his adrenaline and said, sternly, to his reflection in the rearview mirror, "Man, you've got to get a grip. Maggie would have your ass if she knew what you were thinking." He swerved into the driveway and parked behind Maggie's car. Slamming the door, he started up the drive towards the house, talking to himself.

Maggie opened the door, mouth open and ready to speak. He reached out and put his hand over her mouth, saying, "I know. I'm a jerk and a pig. You have the right to talk to Randy about your mother, and I'm sorry, ok?"

Maggie nodded, and Zeke took his hand away. She smiled and said, "Thanks. Now that we've got that settled, I think the first attraction is starting." She stepped back, and he entered the house, not unlike a prize fighter re-entering the ring after a victory. She shut the door.

Nick Benson watched from the bushes as the two forms embraced briefly then went towards the back of the house. He began to make his slow way to the windows where he could see them. He settled in a full spread bush and watched them cuddle on the couch.

Bart, he mentally sent, *I feel like a pervert! Is this absolutely necessary?* Shifting around, he found a spot that afforded a good view of the couch and the lovebirds. He hoped the lone police officer didn't drift by and catch him 'peeping.' That would just suck all the good intentions right down the proverbial drain.

Damn straight, Nick. I don't care what your personal feelings are. Maggie needs your help, and so does Lilly, if it's not too late. Do you understand? Bart's deep voice boomed in Nick's head so loud he winced.

Yeah, yeah, Nick thought disgustedly. *I just wanna know how doing something so good can feel so wrong.* He shivered a bit, trying to rest comfortably while he spied on his targets.

That, my friend, is the name of the game. Bart laughed in Nick's head. *Just keep me posted, alright?*

Alright. But if it goes any further, I'm closing my eyes. Nick shifted his weight again so he'd be more comfortable. It could be a long night.

Inside, Maggie snuggled into Zeke's arms. Nick sighed, but diligently watched as ordered.

CHAPTER

FIVE

Maggie was running her heart out, trying to catch her mother. The night closed in around her, the darkness seemed oppressive. Tendrils of fog swirled around her legs as she ran. She couldn't see the ground, but could hear her footsteps thud on the path in the quiet. She could see her mother just ahead on the path; the faster she ran the further away her mother seemed to be. She began calling to her, putting more and more volume to her voice until she went hoarse. The only recourse was to run faster, and she did… running, running…

"Maggie! Wake up!" Zeke shook her. He lay a hand on her thigh and squeezed.

"What?" Maggie bolted awake. The fog from her dream clouded her vision. She blinked. The soft glow of the TV screen lent an eeriness to the familiar surroundings, bathing the den in an alien light. Panic surged in her chest. "Where am I?" She shook her head, running her fingers through her hair.

"In the den. You were dreaming, I think," Zeke said, leaning forward and lighting a cigarette. He grinned to himself and lay his Zippo on the cigarette pack.

"I'll say. What a weird dream." Maggie shook her head. "I was chasing my mother. She was just ahead of me, and I couldn't reach her. Strange, huh?" She glanced at him and caught the smirk before he could undo it. "Why are you smirking like that?"

"Yeah, it's strange." Zeke flicked his cigarette towards the ashtray. The ash missed and splattered on the table. Zeke scooped it into one hand with the other and dumped it in the ashtray. "You were calling her in your sleep." He glanced at his ash again and flicked the cigarette over the ashtray. "I was grinning because running your fingers through your hair totally destroyed your hairdo."

"Oh. Was I?" Maggie asked, confused. "Huh. Don't think I ever did that before." She ran her hands through her hair again, and said, "Called to her in my sleep I meant."

"Don't you remember your dreams?" Zeke looked at her, then away. A lock of hair fell in his eyes, he wiped it away. "I do." *Now that is an interesting 'do* he thought to himself. He kept his eyes away from her hair before his sense of humor got him in trouble again. He knew better than to say it out loud.

"I don't. At least, I didn't used to. I mean, I don't think I ever did." Maggie stared thoughtfully at the television. A commercial played out while she stared uncomprehendingly at it. "I can't remember."

"Well, I don't think it matters much. A lot of people don't remember their dreams. Maybe you should write it down." Zeke went over to the desk under the windows and picked up a pad and a pen. Coming back he handed them to her.

Taking them, she looked up at him, and he flushed. "Why?"

Zeke glanced at the TV, then her, then back to the TV. Sitting down next to her, he said, "Some people say that our dreams contains answers to questions that we have. Our dreams guide us on our life's journey, and contain the instructions we need to fulfill our destiny. That's according to dream therapists." Zeke ground out his cigarette. "Metaphysicians say that dreams might contain the stigma of prophecy.

Me? I don't know. But it's worth writing down anyway, especially if you can't remember having dreamt before. There's bound to be something significant in it."

"I never knew you were so deep. You've surprised me." Maggie picked up the pen and opened the notebook. She wrote out her dream while Zeke read over her shoulder.

"Put in everything you can remember. What the atmosphere was like, the weather, how far away she was, what she looked like…everything." Zeke broke off when he saw the look on her face. She was staring at him like she'd never seen him before. He flushed again, and stammered, "Well, you never know what part of a dream is important. That's all."

"Do you write down your dreams?" Maggie asked while writing. She looked up at him when he didn't answer, pen poised above the pad of paper.

Zeke was staring at the TV, seemingly lost in the movie now that it was back on. So softly that she could barely hear him, he said, "I keep a dream journal."

"Oh." Maggie went back to recording her dream. *You learn something new every day*, she said to herself. She was suddenly very conscious that he was next to her.

Randy gripped the steering wheel so tight his knuckles turned white. "I still don't see what's wrong with you, Lilly. Every time I say something to you, you glare at me." He glanced around. The park was deserted. Dark gray silhouettes of park benches made lighter blotches in the moonless night. He'd driven here in hopes of talking some sense into Lilly, but so far all they'd done is argue. Fleetingly, he thought, *A week ago, I'd be trying to make a move on her.* Now, a lone street lamp tried vainly to brighten the park, but was failing spectacularly, and he was wondering what he was doing there. Things felt so *wrong*.

"And I've told you every day for the last week that it's not you, it's me!" Lilly shouted, slapping the dashboard with a resounding *smack*.

"How can I tell you what's wrong with me if I don't even know!" Her hair was again tied up in that ridiculous bun, and the clothes she was wearing were skin-tight. A myriad of emotions flipped across her face, finally settling on a look of hopelessness.

"At least tell me what you're feeling," Randy said, almost pleading. "Something is going on, and I would like to know what. You were an attractive woman who dressed and acted professionally when we first met. Look at you now." He looked over at her. She was staring at the dashboard, sitting quietly. "Lilly, I would think you were having an identity crisis if I didn't know you better, and frankly, your behavior recently causes me to wonder if that's what's going on with you. You are not the woman I met a few short months ago. You dress like a hooker, you're hostile and uncooperative, and you're alienating Maggie. Do you realize that?" Randy could hear the desperation in his voice. He didn't realize how much he cared for her until just now.

"I know I am, and I don't want to. I wish I knew why it is happening," Lilly said, softer. "I love her, Randy, you know I do. She's my daughter, my life, my one and only precious child, but every time she looks at me, I feel like she's judging me or something." Lilly looked at him, her eyes glimmering. "Almost like I need to explain myself to her. I just can't understand it." She rubbed her hands on her skirt as if she could wipe it off. Her hands drifted up and undid the bun in her hair. She fluffed it out. Her hair cascaded down around her face as she said, "I just don't know how much more I can take. I feel like I'm falling apart, and that everyone hates me." She glanced at him, eyes haunted. "Even you."

Randy looked into her eyes. A stab of fear thundered in his chest. She looked so much like a soul in torment. Patting her leg reassuringly, he went back to staring out the windshield so she wouldn't see the helplessness he felt. "Lilly, you know I care about you." He swallowed and wondered if he should say how much, then decided she needed to know. "I care very much, honey. I can't even begin to say how much. Is there anything I can do to help?"

"No. I think I'm beyond even your help. I'm sorry." Lilly hung her head. A tear dripped off her jaw. "I just wish I knew what was going on. I feel so lost all the time." She toyed with the door handle with one hand. The other gripped the car seat like she was grounding herself to reality.

Randy patted her knee again. He looked at her. Her face was averted; she was staring out the passenger window at the bushes alongside the pathway trailing off into the distance. She lay a hand on his and squeezed.

"I love you, Randy. Tell Maggie I love her, too." She pulled the latch and opened the door. Hitting the door lock, she slammed it shut behind her. The dome light flashed and died, momentarily blinding him as she streaked to the bushes along the path and disappeared within them. Randy fought with the door, finally hitting the lock and leaping out the car.

"Lilly! Where are you going?" Randy yelled, but it was too late. She was gone. Randy yanked out his cell phone and dialed Bart. Maybe it wasn't too late to save her. "She's gone, Bart, and I'm afraid she's running to Iris." Randy struggled with the hopelessness in his chest. Now that she was gone, he knew he loved her. He wondered if it would make a difference. He blinked; he still had faint dots in his eyes from the dome light.

"Damn. We'll have to do something." Bart said, his deep voice projecting confidence. "Lilly is useless to them for the ritual. They need a virgin."

"Right. But if that's true, then why…" Randy hesitated, then said, "I think I see why." He moved the phone from his ear for a second while he contemplated the consequences ahead, then moved it back.

"Exactly. Maggie is now our primary concern. I'll meet you over there," Bart said.

"Alright," Randy said, hanging up. He turned on the ignition and slapped the gear into drive. He hoped they were in time.

Zeke brought a bowl of chips and some dip into the television room and set them on the coffee table. He took several cans of soda from under his arm and put them next to the chips. Maggie, Randy and Bart were all sitting on the couch, Randy and Bart flanking Maggie like they were protecting her from him. Zeke pushed his irritation and his jealousy away; now was not the time. He already overcame his reluctance and raided the kitchen like he lived there; having two men flank the woman he loved seemed ordinary, kinda, now. But only today. He still didn't trust either one of them.

"But what if they really have my mother? What then?" Maggie was saying in a raspy voice as he entered the room. She hadn't seemed surprised when Randy and Bart had knocked on the door. She had even acted like she expected them, for Christ's sake. Bitterness again rose in his throat. He popped a can of soda and drank some of it, hoping to drown the taste. He watched her light a cigarette.

"We'll handle that when we know for sure," Bart said, his voice firm as if to instill confidence. "Until then, there's nothing we can do but alert the police." He pulled a business card from his pocket. "I have a friend in the department, and…" He reached for his cell phone.

"No police," Maggie broke in, her voice dull. Her head was down, and she wouldn't look at any of them. She rubbed her hands on her thighs, slowly down the length and back, like she was thinking. The cigarette smoke trailed up from the butt as it rode along her leg.

Bart nodded. "Whatever you say, Maggie." He glanced at Randy over her head, eyebrows raised, and stuffed the card and the phone back in his pocket.

"She threw the candles away," Maggie said in a dull, flat tone. Her eyes had glazed over, and the ashes from her cigarette fell on the floor. She didn't seem to notice. Bart took the cigarette from her hand and ground it out in the ashtray. She didn't seem to notice that, either. Still, her hands thoughtfully traveled her thighs.

"What's wrong with her?" Zeke whispered. He'd not seen her do that before. A feeling invaded his chest, and he jerked. *I'm afraid*, he thought. His heart thumped almost painfully in his chest.

"Shh! She's channeling," Bart said, excited. "Astonishing." He leaned forward and eagerly, he watched her face, waiting for her to speak.

Zeke groaned. Randy glanced at him and shook his head, placing a finger against his lips. Zeke glared back at him. Randy shrugged and shifted his attention to the girl next to him.

"Duke it out later. I want to hear what she says," Bart said quietly. "It could be important." He glanced at Zeke, then Randy, then back to Maggie. His glance was brief but crystal clear. He wanted silence.

"The candles would have prolonged the inevitable. Lilly was being called to evil," Maggie intoned. "An overpowering voice called to her. There is only one thing that can save her now." Her voice rose in pitch and boomed into the silence. She definitely did not sound like herself. Her hands stopped rubbing her thighs and clasped together in her lap. She sat up straight on the couch.

"We stand ready for enlightenment, vessel," Bart said in an eerie voice. He'd taken out a notepad and a pen, and was flipping frantically looking for a blank page.

Maggie fixed her eyes on him and waited until he found a page. "This one that means the most to Lilly can save her, but the path is difficult to trod. This one must not stand alone." She waited for a second, then said, "Lilly is almost beyond saving. It would take an entire force for good to waylay the evil works afoot. The battle between good and evil has already begun." Maggie fixed her eyes on Bart's face. "This is not news to you, Priest. Thou foresee truth."

Zeke saw her looking at him, and knew it wasn't Maggie. He didn't know *how* he knew it wasn't her, he just *did*. Her gaze made him uneasy and he squirmed under it. Her expression softened, and she turned away when Bart spoke.

"I understand," Bart said, writing. "Thou knowest of my plan, vessel. What think thee of it?"

Maggie stared off into space for a few minutes, then roved her eyes back to Bart. "Much of their doings are hidden from me by a great evil. You must prepare for this most carefully. This evil will destroy you utterly if given even half a chance, and it is close to halfway already." Her fists clenched in her lap, and she started. She heaved a great sigh and her shoulders slumped.

Randy lay a hand on Maggie's shoulder. Maggie turned her head to look at him, gazing at him contemplatively. Randy dropped his hand as if embarrassed. She said, "This one will need your comfort someday. See that you are available." Randy nodded.

Zeke scowled. Maggie turned her eyes on him, and said, sternly but sympathetically, "You must promise to aid Maggie in this battle. She is vulnerable to attack, and only someone with great love for her can stand behind her and help her win this battle. You three are all she has in the coming days, you are her support network." Maggie sighed heavily. "I fear for the mother. I believe she is in despair."

Bart said, pen poised, "Can you elaborate, vessel?"

Maggie closed her eyes and began to rock slightly. Her hair fell in her face, and she made no attempt to move it. She mewled as if in great pain and intoned, "Lilly is a lost soul. She has been lost from the beginning. Everything you've seen of her, everything she's shown to the world has been a carefully crafted façade. Even this one does not truly know her mother's heart." Maggie lay a hand on her own chest. "You three must aid this one to find herself." She lifted her eyes up towards the ceiling. "It is imperative that this one grow into her place and quickly. She is in great peril." She slumped, her head falling to her chest.

"Consider it done, vessel. Thank you for the information." Bart clicked his pen closed and hastily thrust his notebook back in his pocket.

Maggie sat limp for a second and then began to stir. She shook visibly, and opened her eyes. "What happened? Did I doze off?" Her eyes darted around the room, visibly checking things.

"Yep, exactly," Randy said cheerfully. "Are you hungry? Zeke's got potato chips." He nudged the bowl towards her. "There is dip, too." He turned his attention to the movie, as if he had been watching it all along.

"Cool. I'm starving." Maggie took a handful of chips and smiled at Zeke. She glanced at the set, too.

"So, what do we do now?" Zeke asked. He lit a cigarette and blew smoke at the ceiling nonchalantly, as if he hadn't just seen his girlfriend channel another spirit. He watched her carefully out of the corner of his eye. She appeared ordinary. The fear in his chest subsided a little.

Bart smiled at him. "Well, first thing is figure out what to do if Lilly is truly a captive." He helped himself to a chip and assaulted the dip on the table.

Maggie chewed her chips thoughtfully. "If they do have her, what do you think they'll do?" She automatically fed the chips one by one into her mouth, her attention on Bart.

"Lord knows, but it isn't gonna be pleasant. Think you can handle it?" Bart asked, taking some more chips.

Maggie stared off into the distance, then said, "I think so, yeah." Grabbing another handful of chips, she said, "That is so strange. A few minutes ago, I was terrified. Now I think it'll work out. Why is that?"

Bart shrugged, while Randy and Zeke glanced at each other. Slowly the chips and dip disappeared.

Lilly ran like she knew where she was going, even though she didn't. She dodged trees and bushes, sticking to the shadows like a burglar. Her feet carried her past houses and stores, most with lights on, but she didn't look left or right. She just ran.

A figure loomed ahead of her. She called to it.

"Wait up!" She ran faster to overtake the figure, but it always stayed just ahead of her. Occasionally she got close enough to reach out to it, but could never quite reach it. As her frustration grew, she became obsessed with catching him.

Just like a man, she mused. *When you really want to talk to one, they run.* She jogged along in an easy stride, determined to overtake him. She didn't notice when they left downtown. Suddenly she found herself running in a rural area. Large bushy trees lined the road she was on.

"The least you can do is tell me were we are, you jerk! I've been following you for miles!" She shouted. The figure didn't stop. Lilly put out a burst of speed, and so did the figure. They were both all out running now.

Suddenly, the figure came to a dead stop, and turned to face her. She was too close and going too fast to stop. They collided. Lilly went down backwards in a heap, breathing hard and staring up at him. He didn't even look winded.

The figure took its hood down. Lilly stared at what she saw. Her jaw dropped and she screamed. She was still groveling on the ground and screaming like a lost soul when Hakon picked her up. Immediately, she went limp in his arms, and he carried her away into the darkness.

"Listen carefully," Iris said into the phone. "You have only one choice. Come to the red barn at the end of Forest Road alone if you want to see your mother again." Her eyes roved her office. The altar in the corner held, among other things, a smoking black pillar candle, about three inches high. The wax had melted on the inside so there was a pool within the confines of the candle, and the lights in the room reflected in the melted wax like eyes. Even though there was no movement from the floor, the candle moved enough so that the ripples in the wax made the "eyes" appear to wink at her. That bothered her enough that she did not hover over the altar when the candle was lit.

"How do I know you'll let her go if I come?" Maggie asked in a controlled voice. She did not trust the voice on the phone. Everything within her was telling her it was lying.

"You don't. You only know you won't see her again if you don't show up," Iris said sarcastically. "Don't mess with me, kid. You'll lose." Iris slammed the phone down. She fixed her gaze on Lilly. "Don't worry, Lilly. I'll let you go soon," Iris said harshly.

Lilly was dressed in the ritual slave garb; white robe, slit from bottom to waist on both sides and slit from neck to waist in the front. Held closed by a belt, the robe was designed for easy access during rituals without having to be removed. Lilly was naked underneath, like all slaves were.

"When?" Lilly pleaded, her hair in her face. She cowered in a corner, her ankle chained to a ring protruding from the floor. Her eyes held the look of someone on the brink of madness. Every once in a while she gave the short chain a yank, just for testing purposes. She didn't really expect it to come loose; it hadn't so far, but she had to test it. It gave her about a three foot radius, just enough to reach the wall and sit up against it.

"As soon as you don't need the restraints. Sooner or later, you'll like it here and won't want to leave. Especially when your daughter joins us." Iris leaned back in her chair, watching Lilly yank on the chain.

"Is that what you want? My daughter?" Lilly asked, shaking her head so her hair fell out of her face and she could see Iris clearly. She dropped the chain with a clank, and sat back against the wall, knees up and in front of her. She wrapped her arms around her legs and stared at Iris as if daring her to come closer.

Iris got up and walked to Lilly's side. "Hard to believe you're my twin. I thought we'd look more alike." She hunched down and searched Lilly's face for a resemblance to herself. "You've gotten fat on the finer things in life. What do you weigh now anyway?"

Lilly said nothing, just glared at Iris.

"Ah, defiance. That's good," Iris said. She stroked Lilly's hair, and said musingly, "I've always kept my hair short. How do you stand yours so long?"

Lilly jerked away from Iris' touch. The chain went tight, so she couldn't move far. She glared at Iris and remained in her position against the wall.

Iris smiled at her. "The dream that brought you here was real. I planted it in you, that's true enough, but that means nothing." She walked back to her desk and sat down. "I think I'll just leave you there for a while. Maybe you'll be more appreciative of my good nature, eh?" Iris tapped away on her keyboard for a minute, then pushed the intercom on her desk. "Jinx?"

"Yes?" David's voice came through the box on the desk. "What can I do for you, priestess?"

"Come in here, will you? I have a job for you." She tapped more keys.

The door opened almost immediately, and David walked in. His robes swayed as he walked, and he glanced at Lilly before stopping in front of the desk and bowing towards Iris. "As you command, it shall be done."

Iris saw Lilly glare at David, and smiled at him. "Is everything ready?" She pulled some papers out of the printer and tapped them on the desk so they were all together in a neat pile. She set them off to the side.

"Yes, priestess." David looked over at Lilly. "What about her?"

"She can stay there until time for the ritual. We can induct her right where she is, if we have to," Iris said, writing on a pad of paper. She didn't look back up at him, nor at Lilly.

Lilly was staring off into the distance, as if her mind was a million miles away.

"Is she willing?" Dave asked. "She doesn't look it."

"That doesn't matter. Her blood will respond. She can't ignore the call of her nature." Iris stood up. "Come. The two of us shall do it now, then you'll go."

Iris and David crossed the room. Lilly tried to twist free of the chain that held her, but it wouldn't give. She stopped, breathing heavily. "I will never agree," she said, her voice harsh.

"You will. It's inevitable, Lilly. You have always been a part of me. If I am evil, then you are too," Iris said, coming close enough that she could talk normally. "See, we are twins, and what blood flows in me is in you as well. We are half demon, sister. We are evil by nature." A pious look replaced the earnest one. "Blood calls to blood."

"No," Lilly whispered. "That can't be true." Her eyes widened as so many *things* from her past made sense. Like missing puzzle pieces, she saw that one little piece of knowledge fall into those places of her life that always confused and surprised her, and resolve most of them. They lined up like ducks in a row. Her demon blood was the *why* things happened to her. Her eyes widened in surprise. A lot of things. Her mind quickened with her new understanding, and she felt the shift within. *Now is not the time to give in,* she thought wildly. Her attention shifted to David as he spoke to her.

"It is true, Lilly. You are as evil as Iris is," David said, piously, pulling out a Bowie knife. He unlocked the chain from the floor, and pulled Lilly from the room by it. She dug in her heels and pulled back on the chain. David jerked the chain, and she came flying forward and sprawled face down on the floor in front of him. He laughed. Kneeling, he flashed the Bowie in her face. Turning it in the light, he saw the reflection of it in her eyes and said, "Come nicely now, Lilly. I would hate to use this. You have *such* a pretty face."

She sobbed. He helped her to her feet, and led her from the room with an iron grip on her elbow. Her eyes were locked on the knife in his hand. Iris followed them, grinning, and shut the door behind her.

"I don't want you to go," Zeke said. "At least not alone." He sat on the edge of Maggie's bed, his legs just long enough to rest his feet flat on the floor. Her room looked so strange with him in it. He looked out of place among the light green accessories.

"I told you what they said, Zeke. What choice do I have?" Maggie said, repacking her purse. Things from inside that seemed important at one time littered the surface of the table in her room. Absentmindedly, she sorted through things, paying no attention to what she put back in the bag in front of her. "They'll kill my mother if I don't go. I know they will."

Zeke leaped off the bed, grabbed her and pulled her against her chest. "I don't want to lose you, Maggie." He pressed the side of his face against the side of hers and closed his eyes, as if filing away the way she felt against him for future reference.

Maggie put her arms around him and squeezed him back. "I'm not going anywhere, silly. But I have to rescue my mother if I can." She pulled away and continued shuffling things around but not adding anything to what had already been packed.

Zeke hugged her again. Tightening his arms around her, he started kissing her neck. "You heard what Bart said. They need a virgin. If you're not…"

"Zeke," Maggie said, pulling away from him. She looked at him lovingly. "I'm sorry, Zeke. I truly am. I would like nothing more. But right now, my virginity is the only bargaining chip I have." She picked up a brush from the vanity and stuffed it in her purse. "You understand, don't you?"

"Yeah. But I don't have to like it," Zeke said, his eyes bleak. He stared out the second story window into the trees beyond. When he looked back at her, his expression was normal again.

"Neither do I." She shuddered, then sighed and looked at him imploringly. "I have no choice, Zeke. You know that."

"Yeah, yeah." He flopped on the bed and leaned on an elbow. "The way she's treated you lately, I don't know why you would even want to rescue her." He pulled one of her pillows out from under the Hawaiian breadfruit quilt on her bed and stuffed it under his shoulders. He picked at the designs in the quilt without really looking at her. His mind was thinking furiously about how he w\could stow away without her seeing him. *If his presence wasn't in her mind, they'd never know...*

"That is not fair." Maggie sat on the edge of the bed and looked at him. "No matter what she's done, she's still my mother, and I love her. I can't even imagine *not* going." She stood up. Slinging her purse over her shoulder, she said, "After all, what kind of daughter would I be?"

She stared off into the distance for a second, then back at him. "I'll see you later?"

"Yep. I'll be right here," Zeke slapped the bed.

Maggie backed from the room and gently pulled the door closed behind her. She had the feeling it would be a long time before she saw it again, and felt a pang of longing for the happy childhood she'd lived in that room. She felt things shift within her, like a bolt snicking into place, and knew that even if she did see her room again, it would not be the same. Ever. She walked quickly to the front door, her pace getting faster until she was running. Just as her tears started to fall, she closed the door behind her.

Lilly was led to a dark circular room in the bowels of the building. She knew that somewhere overhead was a ceiling, but she couldn't see it in the gloom. Actually, she couldn't see any ceiling at all. There seemed to be a teeming fog overhead. Fascinated, she watched the endless movement before dropping her gaze to the rest of the room.

No windows. Four lit torches decorated each corner, but otherwise the room was devoid of furniture. A huge circular marble slab graced the center of the room, on a sturdy pillar and complete with a gold etched pentagram design, that stopped just shy of the walls on all sides. Short brick walls lined the outside of the circle, encasing the circular slab. The pillar sat smack in the middle of the circle. The air in the room was heavy and smelled of incense. Lilly wiggled her nose, she felt like she was going to sneeze at any moment.

"This is the altar room. You'll get used to the smell." Iris tugged a black robe over her sister's head. As Lilly's face emerged, Iris said, "Your daughter is on the way. I can feel her coming. Can you?" Iris tugged at the robe until it fell right, and picked up Lilly's chain.

Lilly closed her eyes. "No." She actually felt nothing, like she wasn't even inside her own body. *Lights on, nobody home.* A part of her, the terrified, horrified child within, began to laugh hysterically. Opening her eyes, she looked directly at Iris. "Why are you doing this?" Good! Her tone was devoid of emotion. Nice and flat.

"You're the one who says she's psychic." Iris flicked the robe into place and stepped back. "You'd think you'd have figured it out already." Looking Lilly over, she said, "Believe me, I'd rather not be doing this. I'd love to take the place of honor in this ritual, but I can't. I am too close to the source, and it would never work." She smoothed down the long blond hair Lilly still had, and the memory of her fingers doing the same to her own hair flickered then died in her own thoughts. She wrenched her thoughts back to the task at hand.

Lilly said, "What makes you think I can do it, then? If I am truly your twin, I have the same blood you do." Her hair cascaded down over her shoulders, surrounding her like a shining golden halo in the darkness surrounding her. The effect was quite stunning.

Iris tore her eyes away from the vision her twin presented. "True enough, plus you are not a virgin. But your daughter is, and she is the one I want," Iris said, lighting a black candle and placing it in the middle of the floor. The flame flickered wildly, and tendrils of smoke drifted up toward the ceiling. She looked back up at Lilly and said, "Hakon is the one who wants her, I should say." She stood up again and gripped the chain tighter.

"Who's he?" Lilly asked, trying to rip the robe off. The seams of the robe had disappeared. No zipper, no opening. Belatedly she remembered it was a pullover. "Some weirdo you've got hanging around here?" She went to pull it up so she could tear it off.

Iris raised a hand, and Lilly stopped fighting. She became calm. Only her eyes sparked with defiance. She tried vainly to move of her own free will. Her thoughts twitched and thumped against the windows of her mind like a bird trying to escape a cage, but her body did nothing.

"Hakon is our leader. He is also our father," Iris replied. "Ready, Jinx." She held the chain out.

David came close to Lilly, taking the chain and placed a hand on her shoulder. He smiled at her.

She glared at him. He backed off, standing a little ways off, like he was waiting for something.

Iris waved the smoke from the candle towards the ceiling, and began to chant:

> *Your wayward daughter has come home*
> *Forevermore may she cease to roam*
> *Hakon come and bless us strong*
> *So your work can carry on*
>
> *Again I wish to hear your voice*
> *Enfold this one not here by choice*
> *Turn twelve to thirteen, make her one*
> *So your noble purpose can be done*

Iris chanted this again as a swirl of blue smoke formed from the candle flame. In a burst of red-tinged smoke, a shrouded figure materialized before them as Lilly shouted, "How can you do this? Damn it, my daughter is your niece!" The figure threw back its hood, and Lilly screamed. The face from her vision! Her mind froze.

Iris turned to her. "Yes. This is the face in your dream. Meet Hakon, our father." She bowed to Hakon, dropping to one knee before him. He looked at Iris prone before him, and sighed.

"Lillian. My daughter. We meet face to face." Hakon glided across the floor and cupped Lilly's face with his hand so she'd have no choice but to look at him. His claws reached up to her hairline. She cringed from him, closing her eyes and shivering. He blew in her face, and she slumped. He caught her, caressed her face, and laid her gently on the floor.

Stepping back, he gestured over her. Orange smoke hovered over her chest, circling like Indians surrounding a wagon train, before slowly sinking in. She bucked against it, and the candle flame flickered. He said, "My daughter, at last you have come home. Stop fighting me, Lillian. You belong to me, you always have. Let this be as a gift between us." He closed his fist, and the smoke disappeared into Lilly's chest. She lay still.

Turning to David, he said, "Jinx. Take her from this place, and put her someplace where she can rest. Have someone watch her. She will awaken before the ritual tomorrow. When she does, address her as 'Charisma' and do whatever she says. Do you understand?" The atmosphere in the room grew heavier.

"Yes, Lord." David nodded, and bent to pick Lilly up from the floor. He flicked his robe out of the way and squatted next to her. He had just placed an arm under her shoulders when Hakon said, "She is not for you, Jinx. Do you understand?"

David's expression hardened, and he said, "What if I am what she wants?" He went to lift her and couldn't. It was as if she weighed a thousand pounds. He tried again.

Hakon laughed and clenched his fist at his side. David jerked away from Lilly and fell to the floor, screaming and writhing in agony. Hakon let him struggle for a moment, then released him. David sat up, breathing heavily. Slowly he got to his feet and staggered to the wall. He stood trembling against the wall, wary eyes on Hakon. He didn't even look at Lilly.

"Just a sample of your fate if you disobey me," Hakon drawled. "Now go, and do as I command. Keep in mind the same fate and much worse awaits you if anything happens to my granddaughter, whether by your hand or not." He waved dismissively and turned away.

David picked Lilly up off the floor and carried her from the chamber. Her long hair bobbed with the motion of David's gait, her long legs dangled off his other side. She was too long to fit straight through the door, so David turned sideways and carried her off into the recesses of the Coven.

Hakon watched them go, flexing his fingers. Turning to Iris, he said, "You've done well, my daughter. If all continues as planned, we'll see each other tomorrow." He waved his hand and disappeared.

Iris snuffed the candle and walked thoughtfully from the altar room. Her blood was already pumped for the ritual tomorrow, and as soon as the silly girl showed up, she could get everything ready. She hurried away to find David. It would never do to let things backslide now, when they were so close to victory.

CHAPTER SIX

The barn was dark, but Maggie forced herself to go in anyway. Stealthily, she opened the door just enough for her body to slip in, and let it close softly behind her. Her intentions were to feel the place out before the confrontation but she no sooner felt the latch snick home when a voice said, "Ah! Maggie. I am so glad you came."

"Mom?" Maggie blinked, trying to force her eyes to see through the gloom. Sounded familiar but not. The gloom was lightening but not quick enough.

"Not quite," the voice said, as if in agreement. A flare of light blinded Maggie, and she threw her hands over her eyes. In a few moments, as her eyes adjusted, she took her hands down and stared at the shrouded figure in front of her. "Nice to finally put a face with your voice, Mags," the figure said, throwing its hood off.

Maggie gasped. Her eyes widened, and she stammered, "You look just like Mom." She glanced around the barn, and was surprised to see it actually appeared to be a barn. The stalls looked lived in, hay was strewn everywhere, a lone shovel leaned up against a stall down the way, water lipped every watering tank on the wall. It looked lived in, but there was no smell of animals.

"I should hope so. She's my twin," Iris said. She moved away from the lantern on the floor, and faced Maggie, arms folded across her chest.

Seeing her niece's interest in the barn, she gestured sweepingly and said, "For appearances sake. The only animals we have are our familiars." She grinned. "Mostly cats. They don't really care that much for barns until the rats come in from the cold." She chuckled. "Then it's a little free for all. Very amusing, actually."

Maggie felt her hands start to sweat, and wiped them nervously on her jeans. "You can let my mother go now. I came." She forced her hands to lay still at her sides. They balled into fists of their own accord, and Maggie felt that *fight or flight* ping in her chest. All of her senses were heightened. One BOOM and she'd be on the ceiling hanging from her nails. A cartoon cat popped into her head showing just that scenario and she forced it away. Her eyes never left Iris' face.

"Right to the business at hand, I see. As you wish." Iris nodded. "True. You did come. For that, I thank you. It would have been a painful experience if you hadn't." Iris cocked her head. "Would have been a great pity, too. Losing a sister just after finding her." Iris tsked, and shook her head. "I might even have been heartbroken. One never knows."

"You would have killed her?" Maggie said, hating the tone of fright in her voice. Grief snaked into her head and she forced it away. *Later.* Now was not the time to show weakness. Appearances were everything in these sorts of negotiations.

"Not me, child. I order life taken; I never take it myself." Iris smiled at Maggie, and Maggie shivered.

Maggie could feel the anger building in her, but forced it to subside. Standing taller, she said in a strong clear voice, "So what do you want of me?"

"You should already know. Don't tell me Bart is slacking off in his old age." Iris' face showed her surprise then she laughed. "He didn't tell you?"

"Tell me what?" Maggie asked, mystified. ""You know Bart?" Instantly, her heart lurched. She *knew* there was a whole host of things she didn't know or realize, and also knew for a fact that those things put her at a disadvantage. She replayed the events related to her situation in her head, noticing the holes in them; those things that just didn't sit right at the time but she just couldn't see it or feel it. *Hindsight really IS 20/20,* she thought. She prayed for strength and wrenched her attention back to Iris.

"An old adversary. Very well, then, I'll fill you in." Iris gestured towards the back of the barn. "This way." She started walking towards the back but stopped when Maggie didn't follow. She turned back towards the younger woman.

"Aren't you going to let my mother go?" Maggie said calmly, staying where she was. "I'm not going anywhere until I get an answer." Privately she was proud of herself and her ability to sound calm, cool and collected when she really wanted to rip the place down with her bare hands. Maggie could almost hear the gears running in Iris' brain as the woman stared at her.

"Your mother is not going anywhere until you've heard what we want and answered our question," Iris said, gesturing again. "End of that part of the discussion. The sooner you come, the sooner this will be all over." Iris turned and started walking. She didn't look back.

"Very well." Maggie followed Iris further into the barn.

"I don't like this one little bit, Bart. If you've got a plan, now is a good time to tell us," Randy said, cracking his knuckles. The sound was like gun shots, even with the TV on. He fidgeted, absently moving around and touching things, as if straightening his life around. He knew he was nervous, and it showed.

Zeke and Bart stared at him. The television droned on in the background, but none of them were paying attention to it. Zeke smoked one cigarette after another, stubbing out one and immediately lighting another. His eyes darted between the other two men. Bart watched him, obviously thinking.

The three of them were in Lilly's living room. Cans of soda and mugs of coffee littered the coffee table amidst the tissues and magazines and remotes. Maggie had gone to meet Iris about an hour before, leaving Zeke alone in the house, and Randy had joined him a few minutes later. The two had mutually put aside their differences in light of the present situation, and had pretty much buried the hatchet. Bart had arrived shortly afterwards, and the three of them had been discussing their options since.

Bart cleared his throat. "Fine, Randy. You are right. It's time." He sat forward, leaning on his knees with his elbows and said, "Zeke, what I am about to tell you very few people know. Understood?"

Zeke rolled his eyes. "Yeah." He stubbed out his cigarette and lit another one. Blowing the smoke towards the ceiling, he said, "Lay it out, man."

Bart glanced at Randy, back to Zeke, then said, "Very well." An echo sounded in his head, he cocked it to listen, then shook it off. "How much do you know about this town?" *Light just flipped on,* he thought. *Someone's tuning in.* His urgency peaked and he knew time was of the essence.

Zeke shrugged, "As much as the next guy, I guess. I was born and raised here, if that's what you mean." He flicked his cigarette in the ashtray, took a drag and blew smoke at the ceiling. He glanced at Bart to see if that was the wrong answer. He had a feeling that wasn't what Bart wanted to know.

"That's not exactly what I meant, but it's nice to know." Bart confirmed. He sat back on the couch, crossing his legs. "Specifically, I guess I should have asked *what* you know about it's history, not how much."

"I have absolutely no clue where you are going with this. I don't care about history. I hated that subject." He raked his fingers through his hair. "What's with the third degree? It's a town, just like anywhere else, right?" Zeke said, an edge of irritation in his voice. "I just live here, dude."

"A town, yes, but not like any other place on earth, Zeke. Trust me on this." Bart help up a hand as if to ward off further comment. "Let me ask you one more question, then it will be your turn, ok?"

"Fine." Zeke stubbed out one cigarette and lit another. He threw the smoldering match in the ashtray and looked at Bart expectantly.

"Do you love Maggie?"

"What kind of question is that?" Zeke said, startled. His hand jumped, flipping the ashtray. Ashes sprayed up and over like a fountain, drifting down and covering a corner of the coffee table. Irritably, he blew them off onto the floor. *Like the big bad wolf,* he thought.

"It's very important. My plan will not work if you don't." Bart said, his brown eyes boring into Zeke's blue ones. "Please, think carefully. Do you love her?" Bart watched the expressions march across Zeke's face. Bart instinctively knew nobody had asked him that before, except Maggie. Zeke would need time to answer. Bart gave it to him.

Zeke's thoughts raced by so fast he could barely keep up with them. He sped through HER; all her expressions, her scent, her laugh, her ambiance, swallowed and said, "Yes. With all my heart," and blushed.

Bart grinned at him. "Wonderful!" He relaxed a little and crossed one leg over the other, ankle to knee. Resting his hand on his ankle, he rested the opposite arm against the back of the sofa. Randy smiled, too, but his was more of a grimace. Bart registered the look on Randy's face, and winked at him while Zeke was looking away.

"Now, listen closely, Zeke." Bart leaned forward, helping himself to some chips. "About 300 years ago…"

Zeke listened intently, his cigarette forgotten in his hand.

"Don't be stupid, Mags. This is truly the only way to save your mother," Iris said, flicking her robes so they undulated in the still air of her office. A lone candle flickered on the desk Iris sat behind while Maggie perched on a chair facing her.

"I want to see her before I decide. Where is she?" Maggie replied, gripping the arms of the chair she was sitting in. Her knuckles went white. Maggie forced her hands to relax. She felt like she was in the principal's office.

"She is busy at the moment. I'm afraid you can't see her until you're one of us," Iris answered. Nonchalantly, she opened her laptop, and tapped the space bar.

"I don't know, Iris. What you're proposing is hard to believe." Maggie rubbed her forehead. Her head was spinning.

"It's not that preposterous. This country abounds with covens." Iris opened the Internet, and clicked on her favorites folder, then turned the laptop so Maggie could see the list of links. "Just look at all these home pages. Every single one of them is a coven, and they are spread out all over the world. Name a country, and I'll show you a webpage there." She turned the laptop back towards herself.

Maggie stared at Iris for a minute. "I'm not entirely stupid, you know. I know covens exist." She looked resigned. "I just never thought one of them was here."

"Actually, there are two of them here. I lead one, which you are visiting right now." She waved her hand, encompassing the room in the sweep. "Bart leads the Bright Star Coven." Iris said, folding her laptop. "Across town." She threw a calculating look at Maggie. "So, what will it be?"

Maggie's eyes filled. "I guess I have no choice." A tear ran the course of her cheek. She made no move to wipe it away.

Iris smiled. "Wonderful! We'll just get you ready." She slapped the intercom. "Persephone, come in here." She smiled evilly at Maggie. "Welcome to the Ill Wind Coven."

Maggie protested, "I haven't joined anything yet, Iris." Her heart sunk. *Now what have I done*, she thought ruefully. Iris was too happy with herself for her liking.

Iris laughed. "You will, niece. You will."

Lilly opened her eyes, blinking as if to clear them. She looked around the plain room. The only furniture was a single bed, and that was only a mattress and box spring on a frame. A floor length mirror on a stand sat in the corner. No other furniture graced the room. The walls were brick, about ten feet tall, with an open ceiling. Large gold rings were embedded vertically in the walls about 7 feet high. There were no light fixtures anywhere, yet the room was not totally dark. Enough light leaked into the room from the surrounding walls to cast a dusky glow on the bed.

"Hello, Charisma. I'm glad you're awake," David said, sitting on the edge of the bed. His robes draped over his lap to the floor. He held a staff in his hand, and it towered by his side. The ram's head on the tip stared at her with baleful dead eyes, visible even in the semi-gloom. She shivered.

"Is that who I am?" Lilly asked. She ran everything she knew through her mind. "Yes. That is me." She looked down at herself. A white robe she did not remember putting on outlined her shape perfectly on the mattress. She lay exactly in the center of the mattress, the robe spread out on either side. She looked up at David.

"Do you desire anything?" David asked, laying a hand on hers.

"Just leave me. I need to think." Lilly/Charisma pulled her hand away from his and sat up, swinging her legs over the side of the bed. Her robes parted, showing her long legs almost up to the hip. She tugged the robe back into place, but leisurely, as if in a dream.

David's gaze traveled up her legs, past her body to her face. "Very well. I'll be just outside if you need anything." He made to rise, pulling his robe in and bracing his weight on the staff.

Lilly nodded, and said as he rose, "Just remember my name for right now."

"As you ask it shall be." David backed towards the door. With a final glance at her legs, he left.

Lilly pulled herself up and staggered to the mirror in the corner. Staring at her reflection in the glass, she murmured, "Charisma. Why doesn't that name seem to fit me?" She searched her eyes in the reflection but found no answers. Briefly, a sense of loss enveloped her. In her reflection, a blue mist swirled behind her. She turned to face it.

"Father." Lilly's face hardened. "Why have you not visited me before?" She stood tall, the robe sculpting her body. She threw her head up and stood as if facing a firing squad.

"We have much to make up for, daughter, but I will never leave your side again." Hakon said, fully materializing. "We have great plans to enact. Are you ready?" He stood before her, his own robes hiding his shape. He placed a hand on her shoulder, long fingers ending in talons caressing her back and making little scratched circles on her shoulder blade. He dropped his hand from her shoulder and held it out to her.

"Yes," Lilly said, placing her hand in his. "We have much to do."

CHAPTER
SEVEN

Maggie watched the coven members move around stealthily in the dim light from the torches of the altar room. She had been switched from her street clothes to a ritual robe, black with a hood, and was ordered to stand at the foot of the altar stone. A young girl was tied to the stone, one arm or leg fastened to each corner. She lay there quietly, staring up at the ceiling.

Occasionally, a murmuring chant reached Maggie, but otherwise all was quiet. Maggie wondered why the girl just lay there. Why didn't she try to escape? Iris appeared amid a flash of light, standing next to Maggie and staring down at the girl on the stone.

"Obedience. It is time." Iris intoned, waving a hand over the girl's belly. The girl began to struggle against her bindings, trying to get loose. Immediately, five robed figures darted to the stone, two grabbing her arms, two grabbing her legs and one covering her mouth with his hands. The girl began to scream. Iris moved Maggie off to the side, where she could see everything but not be in the way.

A naked male figure loomed in the torchlight where Maggie had been standing, wearing only a carved wooden mask. His skin glowed with a faint sheen and appeared red in the torchlight. He waved a hand at the girl, and her robe flew open, settling in silky folds at her sides. Maggie could hear the man's breathing become ragged. The two figures at the girl's legs untied them and pulled them apart, holding her legs by the ankles off over the sides of the slab, exposing her private parts to the room. Deftly, they tied her ankles down using two golden hooks fastened in the sides of the alter. She struggled and screamed louder, but could not break free. The figure at her head gagged her with a black strip.

The man in the mask watched the struggle for a moment, then lay a hand on the girls' thigh. She bucked, slamming her head on the alter top, fighting her bonds. The masked figure climbed onto the stone with the girl, lifting her hips slightly. Her legs tightened as her hips rose, forcing her pubis to spread open further with the stress placed on her hip joints. He crouched between her legs, hands holding her hips steady and swiftly plunged into her with a cry of triumph. The girl began to scream in earnest and struggle more violently. The masked figure plunged again and again, and the girl shrieked each time and fought harder against the ties at her wrists and ankles.

Maggie closed her eyes and turned her face away.

Iris grabbed her by the shoulders and hissed, "Hide your face, sissy girl, but your ears will hear anyway, and that is what matters." Iris watched the rape progress, the agonized cries from the girl resounding off the walls, and grinned. Her hands dropped. She gripped Maggie's upper arm, and said, "This is a good one. Much more effective than the last ritual slave we had. You should feel fortunate."

Maggie sobbed. She cringed with every scream the girl let out. Iris' soft laughter echoed in her ears. "Why?" Maggie choked out. "Why do I have to be here?"

"This is your initiation, silly girl. After this is over, you'll be one of us." Iris said, her hand digging into Maggie's arm. "You must proclaim to all that your virginity is to be sacrificed for the good of the coven. That is why you must stay. Your words complete the ritual." Iris cocked her head and looked into Maggie's eyes, smirking at finding them closed. "Be glad you are not on that alter. If you weren't Lilly's daughter and my niece, you would be."

Maggie opened her eyes. The shadowy couple on the alter gyrated in the light from the torches, one tightly clasping and assaulting the struggling other. Muffled shrieks echoed off the stone walls. The ropes binding the victim moved as if alive while the girl struggled and was jostled. The girl's tortured tear-streaked gaze rested on Maggie's face for a moment, then was gone as the girl turned her face away and shrieked. Maggie drew a deep breath.

Iris' hands tightened. "Soon, Maggie, soon. Be ready." Maggie closed her eyes again. The shrieks died down a bit. Iris said, "Now, Maggie. Say it now."

Maggie opened her mouth and said softly, "I dedicate myself to the Coven of the Ill Wind."

"Louder. Scream it to the ceiling!" Iris shouted.

Maggie looked up and opened her eyes. The shadow figures still struggled together, their movements frantic in the dim light. She shouted, "I dedicate myself to the Coven of the Ill Wind!" Filling her lungs, she screamed, "If it will save my mother, I give myself to you!"

Her words echoed off the walls, seeming to swirl around the struggling figures on the altar stone. Slowly, the figures wound down - the male slumped with exhaustion and the girl sobbing in earnest. All movement stopped on the alter.

"Very good, Maggie. From now on, the coven will know you as Damaris. You may go now." Iris led Maggie to the door, and pushed her out of the room. Iris closed the door of the alter room, leaving Maggie out in the hall. A draped figure met her and led her away towards the basement. Maggie followed, wiping her tears away with the sleeve of her robe. Not a word was spoken while she walked away.

Zeke snuck through the brush next to the barn. Maggie's car shone in the moonlight with a ghostly glow. Zeke stared at it a moment, then tightened his grip on the knife he carried. A stab of fear stuck in his chest.

Of course you're scared, he thought to himself. Crazy. Witches, covens, demons...what a story Bart had weaved back a Maggie's. Zeke shook his head, willing those cobwebs away. He didn't have time to dawdle, he had a world to save. His own. He planned on rescuing Maggie and making her his, and he didn't care if he had to wrestle a whole passel of demons to do it. But, first things first. Have to rid himself of the fear creeping into his heart.

He sucked in the cold night air until he felt calm. Stealthily, he crept towards the door of the barn. Checking all around, he cracked the door open and ducked in.

Diffused lighting from the ceiling two floors above cast a slight glow in the main room of the barn. He didn't see anyone. He schlepped off to the left, sneaking one step at a time along the wall, trying to stay out of sight in case anyone was looking. From the shadows, he looked over the barn space, trying to determine where he should go next.

Maggie sat in her cell, propped on the bed with her arms around her knees, rocking slowly back and forth, tears dripping down her face, trying to get her feelings under control. She didn't understand anything anymore. The door opened, and she looked up, hastily wiping her face.

Her mother stood in the doorway, but she didn't really look like her mom. Her robe was black, and her fine long blond hair shimmered around her face. She stared at Maggie like a scientist would stare at a virus under a microscope.

"Mom!" Maggie jumped up, facing her mother. Lilly stood quietly, like a soldier at Buckingham Palace, oblivious to her surroundings. The only thing that told Maggie the woman in the doorway was her mom was the length of the hair. Otherwise, Lilly could have been Iris. Fear leaped into her throat, and her joy turned to dread. "Mom?" she stammered, "Is that you?"

Lilly grinned falsely, as if someone flipped a switch. "Why, of course it's me, sweetie. How could you think otherwise?" The grin faded, and her eyes flashed. "I see you joined the coven." She placed her hands on her hips.

"To save you," Maggie said warily. "I had no choice." Maggie watched the march of emotions across the older woman's face. Shock, disbelief, surprise, then acceptance. Lilly closed her eyes, opened them and faced Maggie. Her face hardened. "There's always a choice, Damaris. I thought you knew that," Lilly stated.

Maggie felt her temper rise. "I thought you needed rescuing. Maybe I was wrong. And my name is *Maggie*." She stood straighter, facing her mom.

Lilly moved to the bed and sat down. Patting the bed, she waited until Maggie seated herself, and said, "Not anymore. You belong to the Ill Wind now. This may be difficult to explain, Damaris. I think maybe you'd better listen for a while."

Maggie said, "I'll stand." She rose off the bed and faced her mother, legs wide to steady herself.

"Suit yourself." Lilly shrugged. "First off, my name is not Lilly anymore. You can call me Charisma."

"I used to call you mom," Maggie said, her arms folding across her chest. She knew she was exhibiting defiance with her manner but didn't care. She felt herself pulling her energy in, setting it to swirl within her chest, like a protective circle of light.

Lilly laughed. "Yes. You did. Unfortunately, that woman no longer exists. Even if you did, quote," she made quotation marks in the air, "unquote, rescue me, I would still change my name to Charisma. That's who I am now."

"How do you know? Did Iris do something to you?" Maggie asked, anger causing her arms to clench painfully against her chest. The light within seemed to glow brighter with her distress.

"That would make it so much easier, wouldn't it? To blame your aunt for ruining your life?" Lilly laughed, an evil sound in the small chamber.

"Then what happened?" Maggie demanded.

"I met someone." Lilly stated simply. "A very commanding presence. He saved me." Her face got all dreamy looking, like a teenager looking over a fan magazine.

"I've heard that before, mom," Maggie said. "You said virtually the same thing when you met Randy." Her voice sounded harsh to her ears.

"Randy." Lilly's eyes unfocused, then cleared. "Oh, yes, Randy. He was fun in a human sort of way." Her hands rubbed her thighs softly.

"What else would he be?" Maggie asked, puzzled. "You're not gonna tell me you fell in love with an alien, are you?"

"Far from it, daughter. I finally met my father," Lilly said, her face lighting with joy. "Do you have any idea how that feels?" Lilly got up and paced the room. "I've spent my whole life wondering about my parents. I never told you about being abandoned on a doorstep, did I?"

"No. You told me your parents were dead," Maggie said, astonished. "You lied all these years? Where are they?"

"I was ashamed to admit the truth. It is hard to explain where you come from when the past is hidden from you. My life would have been a lot easier if I had known my origins." Lilly stared off into space for a moment then her eyes settled on Maggie. "So much is clear now. Iris told me of it." She listed events on her fingers. "My mother died while birthing Iris and myself. Our father chose her, my twin, to be the leader of Ill Wind while I was given to the world," Lilly said, her face hardening. "Set out on the curb like the garbage, so to speak. Never adopted, raised by the system. The orphanage chose my last name out of the local phone book." Her face lightened as her thoughts changed. "My father is a wonderful being. I think you'll like him."

Maggie's heart thumped painfully in her chest. She'd heard Lilly refer to other people as 'beings' or 'entities' before, instead of men, woman, or human, but never had the term felt so forbidding before. Maggie took a steadying breath, and said, "Why does the word 'being' bother me so much? You've said it before and it never felt like that. It usually means someone who has passed over. What does it mean now?" She shivered. "It actually gives me the creeps."

"That's not a nice way to refer to your grandfather, Damaris," Lilly said, her eyes blazing. "The creeps. I hope he doesn't take offense to it."

"If you don't tell him, he won't know," Maggie said. She watched her mother warily, not knowing what to expect now from the woman she had once known so well. Again, she wondered what was going on with her mom. This conversation was so unlike anything that had gone on before. Briefly, flashes of good times spent with her mom raced through her mind, only to fade when Lilly spoke.

"The first thing you'll learn about Hakon is that he knows a lot of things. Mostly things people don't want him to know." Lilly answered. She walked over to the door. "I'll leave you now to think about this. Maybe later we can arrange for you two to meet." Lilly flashed a huge grin at her daughter, one that did not make it to her eyes. "Nighty-night." She laughed as she left, slamming the door behind her.

Maggie sunk onto the bed, a scream welling up in her throat. She fought to keep her silence. After a few minutes, she curled into a tight ball, closed her eyes, and began to moan softly.

Zeke watched Lilly enter the hallway, slamming the door shut. Waving her hand over the lock, she murmured something, then walked quickly towards him. He ducked behind a pole and waited until she passed. He listened to her footsteps as she walked down the hallway, then listened as a door opened and shut. Cautiously, he poked his head around. The hallway was clear.

He crept up on the door Lilly had come emerged through. Trying the knob, he found it locked. He switched the knife to his other hand, and inserted the tip of the blade into the keyhole. Meticulously, he began to pick the lock, while turning the knob. After what seemed like forever, he heard the faint click releasing the tumblers, and he opened the door.

He slipped in and closed the door behind him. Maggie was lying on the bed, facing the wall. She didn't appear to have heard him. He moved out of the shadows and called her.

Maggie turned, saw him, and sat up. "Zeke!" She leaped off the bed and stood in front of him, cowering, and looked at him warily. "Is it really you?"

"Shh! Don't alert the masses." Zeke quickly folded Maggie in his arms. "Have they hurt you?"

"No. Not physically. Mentally is another story," she said, sniffling. "I think Mom has lost it, Zeke. She was here a little while ago." She buried her face in the hollow of his collarbone, face tilted up close to his neck. Close enough to kiss it, but she didn't.

"I saw her. She walked right past me," Zeke said. He squeezed Maggie encouragingly. "It'll be alright."

"How?" Maggie pushed away from him. "I'm sorry, Zeke. I just don't know where to turn. My mom has gone all flaky. Remember when I told you my grandparents died before I was born?"

"Yeah. What about it?" Zeke asked, concern making his voice heavy. The look on her face tore at him. He had this wild urge to slay dragons if it would make her feel better.

"Well, it turns out she was abandoned at birth. She says her mother died in childbirth, and her twin sister was chosen to lead a coven. Mom was taken to a local orphanage and raised by them. She was never adopted." Maggie said in a rush. "Now it seems her father is here, and she wants me to meet him."

"That doesn't sound too bad," Zeke said, trying to sound reasonable.

"I'm scared, Zeke. She referred to Hakon as a 'being', not a man. That's wrong." Maggie said, her voice breaking. "Mom only refers to ghosts and spirits as "being". What does that mean?"

"I don't know, baby. But we'll find out." Zeke looked around the room. A single bed on a frame was the only furnishing in the room against the bare brick walls. *Not a lot to work with*, he thought. Out loud, he said, "No windows. Looks like we'll have to sneak through the whole place to get out."

Maggie dropped onto the bed, tears running down her cheeks. "All this was for nothing." She sniffed and hung her head. Tears dripped onto her lap and she sobbed.

"Things like this are never for nothing, Maggie. You've got to fight if you want your mother back. It's the only way." Zeke moved to her side, and sat next to her. Wrapping his arms around her, he said, "Your mother is just lost, baby. We can still save her."

"How?" Maggie looked into his eyes, a few short inches from her own. "How can we save her?"

"I know you've been initiated, Maggie, " Zeke blushed, "But I have to know if they've touched you." He blushed again.

"What do you mean?" Maggie asked, confused. They had held her captive but not hurt her. "They have not harmed me at all. I think they are saving me for something but not sure what."

"That is good to know, but I still need to ask." Zeke cleared his throat, and blushed again. "Aw, hell. There's no other way to say this, so I'll just spit it out. Are you still a virgin?"

"Yes, of course I am," Maggie said, her anger rising. "Are you going to pull that jealousy thing again?"

Zeke sighed, and Maggie's anger subsided. He said, "It's not like that, Maggie, I swear it. You should have figured out that Iris wants you because you're a virgin."

"She did make me swear to dedicate my virginity to the coven. I still don't know why." Maggie ran the recent events in the altar room through her head, and blushed. "Iris made me watch a…I can't even say what it was, but it was sexual."

Zeke shushed her as footsteps hurried past the room. He listened while they passed, then whispered, "I have something to tell you, Maggie, and it's going to be hard to hear, but you've gotta know, ok?"

Maggie nodded. "Ok."

"Bart told me all about Iris and what happened about 300 years ago. This coven tried to raise a devil, but failed miserably. Every 37 years they try again. Thirty-seven years ago the result was your mother and Iris. Apparently, the ritual requires a virgin to mate with an evil entity, some kind of demon, and the result is supposed to be a demon child. The Antichrist." Zeke said in hushed tones. "According to Bart, your mother and her sister are half demon. Their mother, your grandmother, was used in a ritual to raise this demon. When the children were born, your mother was rejected because her blood was mostly human. Iris had just enough demon blood to be useful, so she was retained here. Your mother was sent away to be raised in that orphanage."

"If that's true," Maggie said, her throat constricted, "then I am part demon, too."

"Yes." Zeke said. He tilted her face so that she had no choice but to look at him, and wiped a tear away. "One quarter demon. But that makes no difference to me, do you understand?" She nodded and sighed heavily.

"How does Bart know it's my mother?" Vaguely, Maggie remembered Iris saying that both she and Bart led covens in Mirror Lake. "Never mind. I remember Iris telling me about it." She dropped her eyes. "So, how long has he been watching us?"

"For a long time, he says. Mostly all your life. Jenny was part of Bart's coven. He told me she hired you because you were a natural witch and have an affinity for plants. Randy is part of Bright Star as well." Zeke said, sheathing his knife. "Bart says both he and Randy have been especially attentive since the anniversary of the ritual looms closer."

Maggie thought back over the last six months or so. Bart's face continually showed up, dotting her memories here and there. Randy's face peppered her memories too. Suddenly everything became clear. "My god. Bart and Randy want to stop the ritual, don't they?"

"Yes." Zeke put a hand on her leg. "Bart and Randy sent me to rescue you, Maggie. We've got to get you out of here."

"That won't save my mom, Zeke. But I know what will." Maggie stood up, and slowly unbuttoned her robe. She had undone three of them before Zeke moved from the bed. His eyes were glued on her fingers.

"What are you doing?" Zeke stood up and wrenched his eyes up to meet hers. He reached out to rebutton her robe. "We don't have time for this, Maggie. We've got to go."

She grabbed his hands and put them on her breasts. Holding him there by the wrists, she looked up into his face, again a few inches from her own. "Make love to me, Zeke. It's the only way." She wrapped her arms around him loosely, her eyes on his, trying to not show her fear over losing her virginity on her face. *I always pictured losing my virginity differently* she thought to herself. She pulled in a breath and strengthened her resolve to carry forward. *For mom* she thought.

Zeke looked down at her face, and groaned. "Not now, please." His body began to respond to her touch. He fought to control the lusty feelings rising within him. His hands trembled as he became more aware of where they were located, and he could feel her arms around him, rubbing his back.

"It's got to be now, Zeke." Her eyes bored into him. "The ritual to complete my initiation is tonight. If I go out there a virgin, we're lost, and there will be a demon child. I don't want that." Maggie said, moving her hands over his and guiding his hands in small circles.

"But what about your blood? Aren't you worried about that?" Zeke said, gently trying to pull his hands away.

"It'll be alright, I know it will." Maggie planted little butterfly kisses along his jawline. Zeke looked into her eyes, and kissed her. Maggie quickly discovered she no longer needed to guide his hands, and gave herself to the moment.

CHAPTER
EIGHT

Jinx walked down the hall towards Maggie's cell, his robes twisting against his legs like always. He sighed. All this was getting too much for him. He'd lusted after Iris for years, now he had Lilly to think about too. The two of them did things to him no mortal man should endure. A vivid image of both of them in his arms wafted through his thoughts followed swiftly by the excruciating pain he'd suffered at Hakon's hands. He shook his head as if to clear it.

Maggie's door swelled on his right, and he waved a hand over the lock. "Opencio," he whispered, feeling the lock snick open rather than hearing it. He knocked forcefully twice, then shoved the door open.

Standing in the doorway, he skirted the room with his eyes. The bed lay mussed but empty. The candle had been left burning, and was now about two inches tall. Nothing adorned the plain stone walls. Maggie was gone.

"Oh, my god," Jinx murmured. Panicked, he rushed into the hall and slammed the door behind him as if he could pretend everything was ok. Panting against the doorway, he swallowed and fanned himself with his hand. An intense hot flash peaked within him. His robe was soaked with sweat in seconds.

Jinx forced himself to stand straight and tall, on his own two feet. Breathing deep, he closed his eyes and began to search with his mind…

Maggie and Zeke snuck along the hall clasping hands. Stopping at every noise, they'd made slow progress, but they were close to the main hall that would lead to the barn above. Zeke stopped just before they would have entered the main room, and Maggie bumped into him.

"Sorry," she whispered.

Zeke turned to look at her and squeezed her hand. "You're not sorry, are you?" he said in a low pitched voice. The room beyond him was softly lit, but no noise emerged from the gloom around them. Their voices, though muted, sounded loud to their ears, and they conversed in whispers just in case someone was listening. Sneaking through a pit of supernatural beings anything was possible.

Maggie could still feel the dull ache of her lost virginity, accompanied by the feel of his arms lovingly around her body, and closed her eyes. "Never," she answered just as softly, and smiled at him.

Zeke squeezed her hand again, and said quietly, "You know, I had envisioned us doing that in a much more romantic setting. I wanted to make it great for you, Mags. I'm sorry it took place like that." He shuddered, elated and ashamed at the same time. "I feel like such an animal."

"Don't. I'm not sorry," she clasped his hand in both of hers. "I had visions of the act itself being different, too, but it was always with you. I'm not unhappy, and we have forever to try it again, right?" She rubbed the back of his hand while clasping it in the other. "There will always be time for romance."

He pulled her closer and kissed her. Releasing her, he said, "It's time to go, Mags. We'll have to come back with reinforcements to rescue your mom." He looked at her face in the semi-gloom. "Is that ok?"

Maggie looked back the way they had come. Tears welled in her eyes as she said, "I guess so. I don't think we have much of a choice. I definitely can't be here tonight." She looked into the room beyond.

"Right." Zeke stepped out into the full torchlight of the main room and stopped dead. He pulled Maggie close to him, and stood in front of her. Maggie peaked out from behind him and froze.

Iris, holding a torch, drawled, "Well, Damaris, aren't you going to introduce me to your boyfriend?" Jinx and a few others stood just behind Iris, their dark robes blending into the gloom. It appeared as if their heads were floating in midair. A few of them had torches and held them up to dispel the gloom around their prey.

Zeke pulled his knife out of his waistband and gripped it tight, facing them. Maggie cowered behind him, trying not to scream.

"Let's see, you're the fighting arm of Bright Star coven, aren't you, boy?" Iris said, cocking her head. "It's…Zeke, isn't it? Or maybe Dagger?" She laughed. "That's right. Dagger it is. You'd think Bart would be more original."

Zeke snarled, "What do you want, Iris?"

"Dear boy! Isn't it obvious? I want Maggie; well, I should say, Damaris now, right?" Iris gestured and the coven members behind her advanced swiftly on Zeke and Maggie. Within seconds, Zeke was disarmed and held captive between two burly coven members. Maggie was yanked out from behind him and dragged across the room to Iris' side.

"No!" Maggie screamed, as she was thrust against Iris. Zeke struggled vainly against his captives, but they held him effortlessly.

Iris laid a friendly arm around Maggie's shoulder. Maggie stammered, "What are you going to do to him?"

"That's not up to me, dear girl. It's up to Hakon." Iris gestured and the coven members dragged Zeke down the hall. Iris tugged Maggie along, and the two women followed the men, Maggie sobbing quietly while Iris grinned.

The altar room glimmered softly in the light from four torches, one at each corner of the altar stone. Zeke could vaguely see the stone platform from where he was chained to the wall. If not for the torches he wouldn't see it at all. He stood as close as the chains allowed and shouted Maggie's name as she was chained spread-eagled to the stone. She fought against her captors as he encouraged her.

Figures in black surrounded the stone, chanting over and drowning out Maggie's cries, as Iris came to stand next to Zeke. "You should be proud of your girlfriend, Dagger. She's going to mother the next generation." Her tone was smug.

Zeke glared at Iris. "She's not a virgin, Iris." He rattled his chains defiantly.

Iris, startled, glared back. "What?" The color drained out of her face. She looked ghostly in the gloom. "What was that?"

Zeke repeated, "Maggie is not a virgin anymore." He stood straighter and smiled grimly at her.

Iris slapped him viciously. "Fool! Do you have any idea what you've done? Hakon will kill you for this!" She stomped away, saying, "I hope for your sake that you are lying."

Zeke grinned to himself in the darkness, but his grin quickly faded as he listened to Maggie's cries. His heart dropped, and he wished with all his heart that he could protect her.

"Enough, daughter," Iris intoned. She waved her hand over Maggie, and Maggie fell silent. Her struggles increased but no noise came from her. Zeke began to pull against his chains in earnest.

The door banged open, and a shadowy figure stood silhouetted in the bright glare from the hallway. "Is the Vessel ready?" the figure intoned. The light from the hallway stopped at the threshold, silhouetting the figure in the doorway but not advancing into the gloom.

"She is, father," Iris said clearly. She was standing at the head of the alter, overhanging Maggie who still struggled against the chains holding her down. Muffled noises came from her.

"I smell another," the voice said as the figure entered the room. The door closed on its own behind him. The gloom descended, and the torches contracted, chasing away the light. The room felt oppressive.

"He is of no consequence, father," Iris answered. Her voice sounded disembodied in the darkness. "Indeed. I had not expected spectators, daughter," Hakon said. He pushed his hood off and shook himself. His skin was azure blue, slightly lighter then the gloom around him. He seemed to grow in the darkness.

Zeke watched his horns lengthen in the shadows of the wall. "My god in heaven," he whispered, his eyes wide. His heart tightened in his chest, and he felt fear sink into his limbs.

"Silence!" Hakon thundered. "Do not blaspheme in my presence!" He shot an arm out towards Zeke, hand splayed. Blue flame shot from his palm and engulfed Zeke.

Zeke screamed. It felt as if he were on fire! He twisted violently against the wall and his chains trying to stifle the flames. Just as suddenly, the flames were gone, and Zeke gagged with the smell of sulfur emanating from his clothes and hair. Maggie screamed from the stone, the spell broken by her distress.

"I'm alright, Mags, don't you worry," Zeke called to her, glaring at Hakon. He rattled his chains.

"Keep that tongue silent, wretch." Hakon growled at him, then turned away. He threw back his head and laughed. "Ah! The stench of hate! A perfect nectar for the occasion." He turned to Iris and said, "Where is your sister?"

"I'm here, father," Lilly said, stepping into the light.

"Good. Come here, child," Hakon beckoned to Lilly. Lilly drifted to his side. Hakon placed a hand up the side of her face in a caress. "Do you give me this gift, my daughter? The flesh of your flesh?"

"Yes. Without question," Lilly answered immediately, her eyes meeting his.

"Mother!" Maggie screamed. Lilly ignored her, staring instead into Hakon's face.

Hakon addressed Maggie, "Be comforted, Damaris. It's not every mother who'd give her daughter to such greatness." He laid a hand on Maggie's forehead. Maggie twisted away from his touch. Zeke shouted from the wall.

Hakon flicked a fireball in Zeke's direction, and boomed, "Silence! Her fate is to submit, yours is to observe." He laughed. "If you still desire her after I'm done, I may leave orders that allow you to foster my son."

Zeke ducked the fireball and shouted, "Leave her alone!" He pulled against his chains and felt one give. He jerked harder and felt it give more.

Hakon waved a hand over Lilly, and bent to whisper in her ear. Lilly slumped to the floor. "Jinx," Hakon mumbled.

David immediately moved to Hakon's side, and said, "My lord."

"Remove Charisma from the room and return."

"Yes, lord." David picked Lilly up from the floor and carried her limp form from the room. Hakon waited until he returned, then said, his voice echoing off the stone ceiling, "It's time. Prepare the vessel." Iris moved to the head of the altar stone and gestured to the surrounding members.

Maggie felt her arms held down and her legs being untied and held open. She began to scream just as someone else she couldn't see covered her mouth with their hands. Tears trickled down the sides of her face as she struggled. Hakon waved a hand over her and her robe flew open, exposing her nakedness to the room. He said almost gently, "Remember your oath, Damaris." Maggie blushed and closed her eyes.

A bright light seared her eyes, and she opened them again. A figure stood in the doorway, but Maggie couldn't see who it was. Hakon shielded his eyes from the light and thundered, "Is it done?"

"It is," another voice answered. The figure advanced, swinging the door shut behind it.

Maggie moaned, and struggled as she felt a hand on her belly. She shuddered as the hand traveled down her body. Suddenly, there was a whoosh and the hand was gone.

Zeke fought the chains around his wrist. The one on the right side had broken four links from the cuff, and he was pulling with all his might against the other one. A figure loomed beside him, its face completely hidden within the confines of its robe. "Cease," it whispered from the darkness.

"I can't," he whispered back. "I've got to save Maggie." He couldn't place the voice. It was at once familiar and not.

"You love her then?" the figure asked, still hiding within the robe. The voice was soft and pitched so that it didn't carry anywhere but to his ears.

"Yes, I do." Zeke whispered reverently, still struggling.

The figure grasped the cuff around his wrist and pulled. The cuff separated, falling with a dull clink to the floor. The figure touched the other cuff and it dropped off, leaving him chain free. "Then go," it whispered, and was gone into the gloom. Very quickly it was lost from his sight.

Zeke could not tell who it had been, but he suspected it was Lilly. There was something wrong with her, though. It both felt like her and not like her, but he had never been close enough to her to tell for sure. Shrugging the feeling off, he began to sneak towards the altar stone. When he saw Hakon lay a hand on Maggie's belly, his emotions peaked into protective rage and he pounced.

Maggie struggled against the hands holding her, screaming Zeke's name. Hakon stood up, Zeke holding onto his neck, and flashed a hand in front of Zeke's face. Zeke fell to the floor like a stone, breathing heavy and glaring up at him.

"Fool," Hakon snarled. "All this for the love of a woman." He stood over Zeke's form and tapped a hoof on the floor.

Zeke watched the hoof, as if unbelieving it's existence. "She is worth it," Zeke panted. Vainly he tried to get up, but it was like he was tied to the floor. He just couldn't rise. His heart lurched and he felt fear again. He never expected to see an actual hoof and realized he wasn't dreaming. This was it. He was either going to win the day or die trying. He felt an overwhelming feeling within, and knew he was ready.

"A feeling you will die with, I'm sure," Hakon said, pointing at Zeke. "I would have let you have her when I was done with her." Bright blue flame shot from his hand and engulfed Zeke.

Zeke writhed on the floor, screams ripping out of him as he frantically tried to roll out the flames. The last thing he heard was Maggie screaming his name, then in a burst of agony and immense pain, he knew no more.

"No!" Maggie screamed. Tears came fast and furious, and she felt her heart shut down. She struggled to get off the altar stone and almost succeeded. "Let me go!" She fought against the hands holding her. "Let me go!" she shouted again, hanging off the edge of the altar and staring at Zeke's prone form. "Let me go to him." She fought against the hands holding her.

"Be still," Hakon ordered. He held his hand out towards Maggie, blue flame swirling on his palm. "You could very easily suffer his fate, Damaris."

"You monster!" Maggie screamed, her voice cracking. "How could you kill him?" She lay back against the stone and glared at the demon facing her. Her rage centered in her chest, bolstered by grief. Even though she had not checked on Zeke physically, she knew he was dead. His thoughts were gone from her mind. A suffocating loneliness engulfed her and she wailed once against the grief and pain in her heart.

"All who defy me die, child. One way or another." Hakon waved a hand around the room, gesturing to all the coven members she could see. "This is not my only coven, girl, but one of many. I will admit this is the only one run by one of my children, however."

Maggie shouted, "I am not a virgin, Hakon!" With an evil grin, she said, "Your ritual is useless." She heard a gasp from somewhere above her head. Immense satisfaction shimmered in her chest, and she sent a thought to that now-broken bond. *For you, my love. All for you.*

Hakon laughed, and said, "I know that, silly girl. The moment I touched you I knew that." He swarmed closer to her face and whispered, "But all is not lost. I have a replacement for you." Maggie turned her face away when he bent down to whisper to her. He straightened back up again and said louder, "Your boyfriend was killed because he had violated my orders. That knowledge is yours to live with."

Maggie turned her face back towards him and he stood up at the foot of the alter. Her eyes drifted towards Zeke, and she hoped he still lived even though the bond between them was silent. A tear fell to the altar surface as her eyes watched Zeke for any signs of life. He did not move.

Hakan's eyes raked the room, stopping at each person off in the gloom as if searching for something or someone. "One loose end remains." He sighed and leaned with both arms on the bottom edge of the alter stone, each one of his hands fisted on the stone. He leaned down a bit and hung his head down, like he was defeated. "You know who you are," he drawled.

After a few minutes of silence, David came into the light, stammering, "My lord! I…"

"You!" Hakon snarled. Drawing himself up to his full height, he said calmly, "I enlightened you of your fate earlier." He held up a finger. It glowed with blue fire in the gloom. He held his hand out, palm up, and watched as a blue fireball formed in his hand. "I can't go back on my word, Jinx. The vessel was your responsibility. Look at the fiasco that faces me now! You should have been more vigilant in your duties."

David began to speak, then stopped. His eyes grew wide and his face blanched. He began to whimper. "No, please, no…"

Hakon tossed a fireball at David. It sunk into his robe. David shrunk within himself, hands clawing at his chest. He dropped to the floor, groveling. Blue fire expanded and contracted around him, as if breathing, completely engulfing him. David moaned with each contraction. Through the specks of blue fire that raced along David's body his exposed skin glowed a brighter and brighter red, as if the fire was scorching him. He sat back on his knees, looking imploringly at Hakon. "Please, lord," he gasped just before his skin turned orange-red and he collapsed lifeless to the floor. Tendrils of smoke drifted up from his body. Hakon threw back his head and laughed.

"I never get tired of that! Now to the ritual," Hakon said, his voice strong in the gloom. It boomed off the walls and banked back into the room, reverberating off the brick walls as if in a concert hall. He clapped his hands together three times, and held them out to the sides as if waiting for something to arrive.

"Father," Iris said, her voice low. The members surrounding the stone started chanting in unison until she glared at them. They fell silent. "We are no longer a full coven, father. Without Jinx, we are only twelve."

"That no longer matters, my daughter. Come to me." He turned his back to Maggie and faced Iris as she moved around the table and approached him. Hakon placed a hand along her face, the bottom of his palm at her jawline. His talons overlapped her hairline. "Ah, my daughter," he crooned. "Long did you serve me well, and for that I will say to your face that never had I a better servant. Thank you."

"What do you mean?" Iris asked, trying to shift his hand. She couldn't move away from him. It was like his hand held her captive, like a magnet to a metal wall. Her heart fluttered, and she wondered what it was. She had never felt it before.

"The coven of the Bright Star has been broken as well, my daughter. They no longer have the ability to stop the ritual," Hakon said, moving his hand down to her neck. His eyes followed his hand to her throat. "Unfortunately, I can't take advantage of that for a few reasons. Number one, my vessel is not pure, so the issue would be more humans. That would not suit my purposes." His hand nestled against her neck like a choker. She tried to move away, but couldn't. He went on.

"The second reason is that even though I do have a virgin available, you are too closely related to me, and the issue would be highly tainted. Our child would be pure demon, my daughter, and that would never do. He would not pass in the human world. That alone makes you mostly useless to me." Hakon caressed her neck, his eyes following his hand as it moved leisurely against her. Leaning close, he whispered into her ear, "The fluttering you feel within is FEAR, my daughter. It's like a gift between us."

Iris swallowed and whispered, eyes wide, "We could try again." She moved her hands up and clasped his arm and pulled. She could not budge it. Faint tendrils of fear settled in her breast. Her heart began to pound. She didn't like fear at all. How debilitating.

Hakon smirked. "Yes, we could, but that would be in another 37 years, Iris. I can wait that long, for I am immortal, but you are not. You are sadly human, my child, and all humans must end some time or another." Hakon began to tighten his hand around her neck, then suddenly let her go. "That is one universal law I cannot change, much as I would like too sometimes. Yet one must do what one must."

Iris put her hand over where his had been and rubbed. Her skin was hot to the touch. Hakon moved away from her into the middle of the room. She felt OFF. She didn't know how or why, but something within her was different. She was positive she wouldn't like it. The feeling within her intensified.

"Release her," he said, gesturing towards Maggie. The hands holding her were suddenly gone. Maggie rolled off the altar stone and fell to the floor. Jumping to her feet, she ran to Zeke, robe streaming behind her. She was not aware of her nakedness, all she could see and feel was Zeke. She pulled his body into her arms and rocked him, her eyes filling with tears. Silently, she began to cry. She didn't even care that her robe was still open as tears dripped on his face. Her grief was a raw open wound in her chest.

Iris felt woozy, and her skin was getting hotter. *Houston, we have a problem*, she thought. An intense desire to giggle maniacally overwhelmed her, and she stammered, "What did you do to me, father?" She staggered and fell against the alter. Pulling herself up, she glowed with an ectoplasmic blue and choked out, "Father!" For a brief moment, she glowed like a lighthouse beacon then POOF! she imploded and was gone. Tiny specks of black ash scattered like raindrops all over the room. Those that drifted into the fire from the torches sparked briefly and winked out.

"I've retired you, my dear." Hakon said, and laughed. He caught a large piece of ash in his hand, and stared at it for a minute, grinning down at it as if looking for the woman it had been, then blew it off and watched it flash and burn out.

He reached out, his arm longer than average, and pulled a slight black robed figure from the gloom. When a wave of his hand, the hood fell back.

Maggie gasped as her mother stood revealed in the light from the torches. "No," she moaned. She could feel her rage, grief, and pain gather within her into a ball and center in her chest, and thunder in her ears. Her thoughts swirled in her head, drowning out the room and it's occupants. She closed her eyes and sobbed into Zeke's hair. Memories of him interchanged with shared moments with her mom, and her heart literally ached with the loss.

Lilly gazed adoringly up at Hakon, ignoring everyone in the room.

Hakon cupped a hand around Lilly's head, hooking his talons in her hair. "Daughter," he intoned, "I'm leaving you here to carry on in your sister's place. We will never be parted. You will hear from me." Blue smoke swirled up from the floor, surrounding Hakon bit by bit until he was engulfed. A stiff wind blew through the alter room, blowing away the smoke. Hakon was gone.

Lilly swayed, eyes closed and face raised to the ceiling for a few minutes. Suddenly screaming, she clutched her face and crumpled to the floor. A few of the female coven members flew to her side, trying to help Lilly to her feet. She shook them off, and stood up under her own power. Opening her eyes, she gazed contemplatively at her coven members. With a gasp, they backed up.

Maggie looked at her mother, barely recognizing her in the gloom of the chamber. Lilly came closer, hunkering down so that she and Maggie were face to face. Maggie choked back a sob, suddenly frightened. Lilly's eyes were yellow and glowed faintly.

"My daughter, this will be the last time you see this vessel, and the last time we may call you my child. The call to follow our destiny is too strong for us to fight, and we have surrendered ourselves to it utterly. Once this night is over, Lilly Wassanbloom will no longer be on this Earth. We will be Charisma now and forevermore, and an enemy to you." Lilly ran a hand over Maggie's head, caressing her hair. Maggie opened her mouth to speak, but Lilly put a finger across her lips and said, "Don't talk, just listen. We have done this for you, Damaris. The part of us that was your mother loved you very much, much more than she ever loved herself. She gave herself to a life of service to the Coven so you could go free. It was she, in her last act as your mother, that set Zeke free so he could save you. You may think on that as a comfort in the days to come."

"But, mom…" Maggie said, tears falling, "we did what we did to save you. All of it was for you."

"Once upon a time, I would have appreciated that, girl. Now it just makes me regret my decision."

Lilly stood up and announced, "I am Charisma, your leader. Remove this girl and her dead boyfriend from my presence, and clean up this room." Lilly shot one more last look at Maggie, then turned and left the alter room, slamming the heavy doors behind her.

Maggie watched her mother leave, and clutched Zeke closer, sobbing. She didn't even feel the hands of the coven on her. Clutched in her hand was Zeke's Zippo lighter. It was the one thing she would never lose.

CHAPTER NINE

Maggie opened her eyes to the inside of her car. Her keys were in the ignition. She glanced over at the passenger side and gasped. Zeke was there, eyes closed, just like he was sleeping, but he was so pale. Maggie caressed his cheek. He was so cold to the touch. She whispered, "I love you, Zeke."

Sitting back behind the wheel, and staring straight ahead, she said, "I will always love you." Maggie started the car and drove away from the Coven of the Ill Wind. From the darkness under the barn, a pair of glowing yellow eyes watched Maggie's car until it was gone.

A few miles away from the Ill Wind Coven, Maggie pulled over and shut the car off. Opening the car door, she leaped out and fell to her knees. Sitting back on her heels, she screamed her grief and anger to the sky. "What am I supposed to do now?" She yelled at nobody. The trees stood silent, and the night closed in around her. Zeke was dead. Her mother was no longer her mother. Jenny was dead, too. How would she live? She was alone.

She sniffed and crawled over to the car and leaned back against the tire. Her legs were straight out in front of her, her hands limp in her lap, and she bowed her head. "Lord, I need you now. I need some guidance. What do I do?" Maggie said, despair in her voice. "I have nobody now."

She let the tears fall. Deep within her, she felt a stirring, like a fluttering deep in her abdomen.

She needed to think, to plan her life from now on, but the things that had already happened were too much to absorb. A small part of her thought about the flutter but she had more immediate things to think about. Like keeping the house up, paying the bills, eating, working, loving, all the things people did every day. Living, pretty much. She had no desire to even think about those things, but she knew that she needed to decide to live or not, and now was that moment.

"Mags. You are not alone. I will always be with you." A voice said, one that she never expected to hear again. "Plus there's another you need to think about."

Maggie looked up. Zeke stood before her, slightly glowing, looking extremely healthy. He grinned at her. She could see through him. Maggie stood up and faced him. "You're dead."

"Yeah, so I have heard." Zeke said, smiling. "I am a ghost now, apparently." He stuffed his hands in his pockets. "I have to admit this was not the way I planned on spending eternity with you, but it's better than rotting away somewhere. Besides, I will be there for our child."

Maggie started. "Child?" She shook her head. Impossible. They had just had one night together and this was that same night. She couldn't possibly be pregnant.

"Oh yes, you are. You are carrying our child, Mags. A girl. Our daughter will be gorgeous, just like her mother." Zeke grinned again. "Comon, my lovely, time to start living again." He extended a hand to help her up then remembered. Looking at his hand, he passed one through the other and said, "this is gonna suck if I can't touch you."

Maggie laughed a bit, despite her grief.

"You have the flower shop, too. Bart already told you that you could buy it. That's your living. Plus you have Bright Star coven at your back. Bart and Randy will help you." Zeke smiled at her, his eyes soft and encouraging. "You are not alone."

He was right. A world of weight fell off her as the phone rang. She answered it.

"Maggie? Finally - are you alright?" Bart's voice boomed into her ear and she held the phone away from her head. "What's happening? How is Zeke? and your mom?" The weight moved back in, suffocating her.

Tears welled up, choking her voice, and she croaked, "I need you, Bart. Please come."

"On the way." Bart said, "I gps'd your phone. I will be there shortly."

Maggie closed her phone and leaned back against the car. While she waited for Bart to come, she planned. Zeke was right. She would make a life for her child. But for now, it was time to mourn, and she let it come. Tears fell for Zeke, her mom, Jenny, even Iris deserved a tear. But mostly, she cried for herself, because she now had to live a life without Zeke and she didn't want to, not one bit.

But, such was life. Or so they said.

THE END

www.ingramcontent.com/pod-product-compliance
Lightning Source LLC
LaVergne TN
LVHW092047060526
838201LV00047B/1271